WINDSOR RED

Jennie Melville

St. Martin's Press
New York

Library of Congress Cataloging-in-Publication Data

Melville, Jennie.
    Windsor red / by Jennie Melville.
        p.   cm.
    "A Thomas Dunne book."
    ISBN 0-312-01846-0 : $16.95
    I. Title.
PR6063.E44W5 1988
823'.914—dc19   87-38245
                                                                CIP

First published in Great Britain by Macmillan London Limited.

First U.S. Edition

10 9 8 7 6 5 4 3 2 1

This book is affectionately set in Windsor but all else is fiction. The town, the Castle and the Great Park are there, but have never known anything like the events I describe. The Garter Procession takes place as every visitor to the town knows, and so does the changeover of the royal party from their cars to their carriages in the Great Park during Ascot week, but everything else is my invention. All the characters are totally fictitious.

J.M.

WINDSOR
RED

Exegesis

Charmian Daniels said: 'First of all, I want you to know that I was in earnest about the research project, that it was not a cheat, as you put it. You were unkind there, Beryl Andrea Barker. I meant it, and I will finish it. Whether I end up with a degree or not is not important to me. I want questions answered.'

Baby said: 'What were you looking for?'

Charmian paid the speaker the compliment of being thoroughly serious. 'I was looking to see if there really was a "feminine" crime, and so a feminist criminology. . . .

'I was seeking something that might be important to all women. Perhaps I wasn't up to the job. I knew the questions, but were there answers for me? I was trying to find out why some women keep on committing criminal acts. And was it anything to do with them being women?'

'And did you?'

Soberly Charmian said: 'I discovered crime is not sexist, although lawyers and the police may be. There is no feminine crime, no feminine cause for crime, women do not turn to crime because they lack husbands or fathers. Not really. There are no essential woman criminals. There are just women who are criminals and they have their reasons.

'Like men.

'The causes of a woman's crime are the same as they have always been. They are unemployed, or underemployed, or they are unhappy. Or they have ambitions.

'Like men.'

'We can do anything,' said Baby, not without pride. 'But some crimes are better than others.'

1

Chapter One

A splash of red fell on Charmian Daniels' white dress like a tear of blood. She looked up in surprise. But it was only a petal from her escort's buttonhole.

He apologised. It was the heat making the rose drop. 'Look now,' he said, pointing up the Castle hill with his programme. 'Here come the Guards. It's the turn of the Blues and Royals this year. Pretty trim, aren't they?' He had an army background himself, among other things, and knew what to look for.

'Yes,' agreed Charmian.

As they were. Immaculate with helmets and accoutrements shining, each man booted, gloved and weaponed with elegant perfection. Close to, they did not look like toy soldiers or characters from *Alice in Wonderland* as she had thought they might.

'Last time I saw the Blues and Royals here was when the Falklands war was on. Made you see through the show here to the professionals they are. They do the job.' He added: 'I went home from here and it was the day the campaign ended.'

A small war, she thought, after Agincourt and Blenheim and Waterloo. Perhaps Waterloo was the decisive battle of modern Europe, it said 'No' with force to the first European dictator.

To the sound of cheering and the music of the military band the Queen's procession wound its way slowly down the hill.

'We don't get the Queen Mother this year,' he murmured. 'Usually comes, but this year I believe she's got another job on.' He would know; it was his function to know.

It was all work. Work for the Sovereign and her consort, work for the College of Heralds marching in their mediaeval garb and trying to look at ease, and work for the most noble Knights of the Garter themselves. A masterly spectacle for the

3

onlookers, tourists and locals alike, but the day's task, even if a pleasurable one, for the main actors. A distinguished sailor was getting his Garter ribbon that day. There he was, unable to hide the happy grin on his face.

She looked up at her companion. Was he here on work at this moment? She knew the answer to that one. Work for him, work too for her in a way.

He had dragged her here to the Garter Ceremony over her protests that it was not her sort of show, she wouldn't enjoy it. That had been dealt with briskly: 'Nonsense, you must come. You must see how it works.' Then a smile. 'Besides, I'd like to take you. And a party afterwards in the Castle. You'll enjoy it.'

An order, was it? Well, probably. But one she was glad now she had obeyed, because, of course, he had been right and she had enjoyed herself. Even standing for about an hour in the blazing sun for a spectacle that was gone in a matter of minutes. She made appreciative noises.

'Of course, you ought to see it from the inside as well, sit out the ceremony in the Chapel,' he murmured with the air of a connoisseur of state occasions. As, indeed, he was.

'I would if someone would invite me,' she said.

As they made their way slowly through the crowd towards a tea-party in the house of one of the Military Knights of Windsor, a police constable gave him a respectful salute. Her companion was a high-ranking policeman. So high-ranking that he was really too grand to be her friend. If that was what he was. Their relationship was complex.

The Military Knights of Windsor were a charitable foundation for old soldiers, founded by King Henry VIII at a time when retired military men had precious little to look forward to, however distinguished their service to their king. Originally they had been a college of pensioners living as bachelors a communal life in the care of a warden. Now, these gentlemen of long service to their Sovereign lived in their own homes with their wives. These houses, embedded in the castle buildings, were full of character. Charmian decided she could enjoy living

4

in one herself. The room she was standing in was lined with dark oak panelling, and furnished with well polished old pieces of furniture that looked as if they had been part of the room since it was built. On the long table among the teacups and dishes of strawberries and cream stood a great silver bowl filled with roses.

She was trying to read the inscription and the date on the side when her host handed her a cup of tea.

'Admiring Molly's bowl, I see.' He was a beautifully dressed, alert old gentleman who was clearly enjoying his own party. 'Clever girl, my Molly.'

'I was looking at it.'

'Know what she got that for? Writing the best historical novel of the year for children. Earned a packet, too. Very useful. That thing over there is a gold dagger, that's a prize too. Crime. Does the lot, my Molly.'

Across the room Charmian saw her hostess talking to Humphrey Kent, the man who had brought her here. Molly Oriel was tall, thin, and as beautifully turned out as her husband, the proceeds of crime, doubtless. Younger than he was, but perhaps by not many years. It was easier for women, Charmian thought, if they knew how to do it and had the right hairdresser. She had been giving some thought to that subject herself lately. It had been a comfort to her to discover that she knew how to manage her appearance better than in her youth. In spite of what some women said, you felt better if you were well groomed. Ask any cat.

Her host followed her gaze. 'Very decent bloke, Humphrey. Served with his father. What a tartar he was. My goodness, you had to watch out. They don't make 'em like that any more.'

'Some people say Humphrey is like his father.' Some people in the Force where she worked, for instance. 'He's not that easy.'

Sir George looked unsurprised. 'No? Can't afford to be, I suppose, in his job.' He eyed Charmian with interest. 'Known him long?'

5

'A few years,' Charmian admitted, not prepared to go any further.

'Not in the same trade yourself? No, you couldn't be. Too pretty.'

'I am.'

'Well, I never. Prettiest policeman I've ever met, my dear. You must come and talk to my Molly. You're both in the same way of business, as it were. Not working today, are you, my dear?'

'No. I've got a kind of study leave, a sabbatical term to write a thesis.'

'A thesis on what?'

'Recidivist women,' returned Charmian blandly. Make what you like of that, she thought. I've been a policewoman for eighteen years, I've been promoted and moved south, I don't discuss my job. Not even with you, my charming sir. And no, I am not pretty, but I have achieved a certain appearance.

'My goodness. Are there a lot of them? Too many, I suppose. Women ought not to be in prison. Not the right place for them at all.' In a moment he was going on to say, nor in the army, nor the police force, nor the pulpit, Charmian thought. He was building up an act of himself as the complete Victorian buffer, except that his eyes were full of humour.

'I don't like them in prison, either. Hence what I'm working on.'

'Another cup of tea? There'll be something stronger along soon.' He picked up a dish. 'Try a bit of my shortbread. I'm the baker. Molly makes the money but she can't cook.'

The 'something stronger' which shortly appeared in tall glasses was vintage champagne. In a lull in the conversation, Charmian took her glass to the window and looked out.

In the golden sunlight of late afternoon the grey stones were warmed and tranquil looking. Not a castle that had ever stood siege, or had tragic memories of the slaughter of attackers and defenders imposed upon it. As far as Charmian remembered her history, Windsor Castle had never come under attack.

6

Briefly, she wondered about the Civil War, but although the white shift in which Charles I had suffered execution now rested as a sacred relic in the Library of the Castle, she could not recall that he had stood to fight in Windsor.

Still, English history was made solid in these stones. Only the name of the royal house had changed, sometimes through violence, but more often through the birth of an heiress.

As Charmian looked out of the window, she thought: It's a township inside a castle that I am looking at. I had not realised so many people lived here in their own community. Not just the Court with its special routines and life, but people like the Military Knights and the soldiers under the Constable of the Castle and the police and all the people who keep the whole place running. I suppose Versailles must have been like this, a world within a world.

Humphrey Kent appeared at her elbow. 'Well? What do you make of it all?'

'I was just thinking that it was a world to itself. Not one I would easily learn the rules of. A long way from my women recidivists.'

'You'd learn.'

'Sir George says you are a very decent fellow.'

'He little knows.'

'I think he does; I said you were very like your father and he only laughed.'

'Did he laugh? George hardly ever laughs.'

'It was a silent laugh, but I could feel it. I think if he'd known me better it would have come right out.'

'And you met Molly?'

'Yes.' Her hostess had extended a warm and friendly hand with a firm grip. There was a lot of power in those beautifully manicured fingers. Seen close to she was even nicer to look at although a little more wrinkled. Charmian, who had had to learn about these things once on a job, recognised that her hair had been cut by a master and that her little silk dress had a couture air. It was the buttons and the set of the neck and the

7

sleeves that gave it away. Once you had seen a sleeve fitting in the way it should then you recognised another when you saw it. A properly cut and correctly draped sleeve is a thing of simple beauty, her mentor had said. Molly had such sleeves and they must have cost her several hundreds of pounds each. Add the skirt and the bodice (those buttons were handmade) and you were probably looking at something not far short of a thousand. Well, three cheers for kiddies and crime.

'What did she say?'

'She said come to dinner when we haven't got such a crush.'

Humphrey appeared satisfied. 'You'll do,' he said.

But in fact, her hostess had said much more to her than that, and Humphrey, who had been watching, knew it.

Without effort Molly Oriel had extracted the information that Charmian had a sabbatical period away from work, that she was researching under the supervision of Brunel University. Which university as Lady Oriel knew was not too far away from Slough, thus Charmian had chosen to rent a furnished flat over the studio of a friend in Windsor, rather than live in Slough.

'Oh, Anny Cooper? Yes, Anny, the one whose daughter has killed her boyfriend.'

Charmian kept quiet for a moment, then she took a deep breath. 'We don't know that yet.'

'He's gone, and she said she'd do him in. I wonder where the body is?'

'There may not be one. Anny doesn't think so.' Anny did, though, in a nightmare way.

'Of course not. I'd be the same if it was my child. I'd keep a tighter grip on the girl, though, than she has. Poor Anny. But a good artist. I've got one of her pots. On the table by the door. All reds and golds, lovely thing. Take a look at it as you go out.'

Charmian had such a bowl herself and knew it came from Anny's red period when she was perfecting the lovely scarlet for which she was now famous.

8

Scarlet like blood. But surely blood and violence could never come near this private enclosed world within the Castle ward?

But there was the image. Liquid blood, dark blood, stale blood, clotted blood.

Royal blood.

Chapter Two

Charmian refused an offer of a lift from Humphrey, but he walked with her to the Castle gate where he said goodbye. The policeman on duty gave them a brisk salute, managing deftly to include both of them in it.

'He'll know you again.' Humphrey spoke with satisfaction, and he bent to give her a kiss on her cheek, a chaste kiss, a public kiss.

'It matters?'

'Of course. This is a special place. . . . Keep in touch.'

'I will.'

'And you have your contact.'

'So I have.'

'You're in a good position to meet him on the quiet.'

'That's true.'

'I'm not sure if he'll be a help but he'll do what he can, he's an ex-cop and it was his tip-off in conjunction with what you had to say that started us off. He just saw a face he knew around the town all the time and wondered.'

And had wondered enough to inform the local police. Two lines of information had crossed, thought Charmian, his and mine.

'Don't let him be a nuisance to you.'

'Could he be?'

'As I read him. A bit of an eccentric. Out of the Force by his own choice. Obviously always been able to turn his hand to anything. Done a fair bit of moonlighting in his time, I'd guess.'

One of the many, Charmian thought.

'Harold English will help there, a good man.'

She was being surrounded by helpers, Charmian thought. Or hemmed in, depending how you saw it.

'Sure you don't want a lift?'

'It's so easy to walk down the hill. Nice too.'

Besides, she wanted to think, and without his somehow disturbing presence. The bowl of Anny's had reminded her of many things, good and bad, happy times, wretched times. Anny had given her the bowl when Charmian's life had looked as though it was downhill all the way. At odds professionally and miserable in her private life, part of it her own fault and part outside circumstances, the bowl with its flame of colour had been Anny's token to her that life could be good again. Some women might have offered a prayer, Anny offered a bowl. It was a valuable bowl on that account, and had come with Charmian on this sabbatical voyage together with her tabby cat called Muff, and those books from which she could not be parted. Keats' letters, *Persuasion* and *The Clever Woman of the Family* (to her mind the best novel Charlotte M. Yonge ever wrote) were now on her bedside table in the comfortable rooms she was renting above Anny's place.

When Anny gave her the bowl, she was the happy one and Charmian the one to be comforted. Now their positions were reversed with Charmian busy setting herself and her life to rights and Anny in crisis. The fact that the crisis was not of Anny's creation made it worse. As Charmian studied the case histories of some of her women prisoners, she asked herself if it ever was the woman's fault. There was usually a man somewhere in the picture who could take some of the blame. But this was the sexist, unscientific thing one was not encouraged to say. She was studying a group of unlucky women and she could see clearly that in many cases the trouble was their relationship with a man. Sometimes a father, sometimes a husband, on occasion a brother, but that male figure was always there. Well, it was part of her thesis to prove or disprove what might only be prejudice.

Only I'm not prejudiced, she thought, avoiding a crocodile of Japanese tourists, doing Windsor today, Oxford tomorrow and the Shakespeare Festival Theatre the day after. I like men. I've

11

worked with them, respected them and had their respect back. But some women ought to keep away from men.

Women like Anny, and even more, Anny's daughter who seemed to have her mother's trouble in a concentrated form. She was Charmian's god-daughter, too, which somehow made Charmian feel worse. I haven't done enough for that child, she thought. I ought to have passed on to her some of the things I've learnt, and all I seem to have handed on is the bad luck I don't need.

She walked on, past the row of dress shops, past the shop selling cheese, until she came to the narrow passage that led to Wellington Yard.

Already it felt like home. She turned into the yard. She could see her cat's face pressed against the window. Muff bitterly resented incarceration, but so well known a wanderer and fighter had to be protected against herself. It was a long way home to Deerham Hills and several alien tom cats had already been seen hopefully hanging round the yard.

There on the right was the baker's shop where you could buy only stoneground wholemeal flour and bread (nothing white or over-refined permitted) and where even the sponge cakes were oatmeal coloured, but tasty and lighter than you would think. Next door stood the wholesaler's for artists' materials like paints and brushes and canvases. You could even buy a picture there, he always had a small exhibition going in the gallery at the back. In fact Jerome was one of the reasons that a colony of artists was growing up around here, turning this area of Windsor into a little Chelsea. Across the way from Jerome's was the dairy selling goats' milk and free-range eggs with the occasional basket of organically grown vegetables. At the end of the yard, facing the entrance to the passage was the range of buildings that housed Anny and her activities. There was Anny's studio and next door to Anny the Theatre Workshop of the local Actors' Co-operative. Anny lived above the shop and, at present, Charmian lived above Anny.

The windows were open in the studio so Anny was still at

12

work; she liked to work in a flow of fresh air. She seemed to find a stiff breeze stimulating. Charmian could see her figure moving round. They had known each other since they were sixteen and were still friends. Sometimes highly critical friends, sometimes angry friends, but always the relationship held. Nothing could break it because underneath it all they trusted each other.

One of the reasons for lodging in Windsor was Anny. Another was Baby: Beryl Andrea Barker whom Charmian had once arrested for armed robbery, and who she strongly believed might have helped kill a man but nothing had ever been proved against her on that score.

Baby and Anny; to have one friend in a new town was good but to have two, the way her life was at the moment, was even better.

Anny was the older friend and the most loved, but Baby was the one she was interested in at the moment.

She considered. Or had been until Anny came up with this terrible problem of her daughter.

Anny poked her head out of the window. 'Your cat's been stamping around and shouting. What a bully. Wants to get out.'

'Yes, she always does.' Charmian hesitated. 'Shall I come in or are you busy?'

'No, come in. Let me see you in your glad rags.'

She's in a good mood, Charmian thought. Perhaps she's had some news about Kate.

But when she saw Anny she knew the news was not good and that this was just Anny putting a brave face on things. Anny's brave face was always heart-rending, like a baby pretending to enjoy the medicine. She was a small woman whom nature had intended to look calm and happy, which was what Anny claimed she wanted for herself but rarely achieved.

'You're working late.'

'I'm preparing the furnace. People don't realise how long it takes to make a good pot. It can take me days sometimes doing the glaze.' She was wearing stained jeans and a loose smock of butcher's blue. Charmian knew that these clothes had been

13

expensively designed to look old and cheap, and that their art lay in making Anny look like a thin person inside her flowing clothes, whereas Charmian knew that her Anny was plump. As students they had both been on a perpetual diet. Now Anny had given up and Charmian no longer needed to. Her metabolism had changed perhaps, or else her life saw to it that she kept thin. Anyway, she could not have afforded to dress where Anny did. Anny had always had money and now she was earning it as well.

Anny looked up from the furnace. 'Good party?'

'I think I could enjoy the life if I got the chance.'

'But you didn't buy a new dress, I notice. I've seen that one before.' Anny appraised the white silk printed with poppies.

'No, indeed. This one did me very well. You are talking to a Scotswoman, don't forget. No point in overdoing things.' All she could see now was Anny's back. 'Well, what is it? Migraine?'

Anny shook her head. 'Got tablets for that,' she muttered. 'Don't get it so badly now, anyway. Fire's dying down inside me. Not so much love around.'

'Oh come on, Anny. What is it?' Who is it was the real question: Jack or Kate? It had to be one or the other. Possibly both.

'Oh you do sound free and uncaring.'

'Not loving anyone either,' Charmian reminded her. 'No one to love.'

'Not even Humphrey?'

'No one could love Humphrey. He wouldn't allow it. And I don't blame him.'

'Not so sure.' Anny closed the door of the furnace, adjusted a thermostat, set a time clock and turned to face her friend. 'I've seen him look at you.'

'So what's wrong? We aren't really talking about me.'

'It's Kate.'

Of course it was. 'You've heard from her?'

Anny nodded. 'Telephoned me. About half an hour ago.

14

Wish you'd been here. You might have been able to trace the call.'

'I doubt it.'

'She wouldn't tell me where she was. But I could hear kind of noises off, sounded like a railway station. Could have been anywhere. And I said: 'Where are you? Where's Harry?'

Charmian waited while Anny drew in a shaky breath.

'She said, "Oh, you'll see him again. Or a bit of him. The bit I let go." And she laughed.' Anny looked as though she might cry. 'That's my own child and I don't know what to make of her any more. I feel as though I've lost her.' Sadly she added: 'I love her though.'

Six months ago Kate, who was an architecture student at Portsmouth Polytechnic, had gone to live with another student, a man some years older than she was, already divorced, a man with one career behind him as a soldier and now starting another one as an architect.

From the start it had been a noisy relationship with plenty of quarrels and more than a hint of violence. This did not matter so much to Anny while Kate and Harry kept it to themselves, although it worried her, but on a day trip to Windsor to show Harry the Castle they had staged a noisy scene in front of Queen Mary's Dolls' House. Kate had hit Harry's face and screamed that she would kill him. His nose had started to bleed and blood spurted over them both. He was a good bleeder.

Violence in the Castle produces a quick reaction and a policeman arrived at once to move them out. Unluckily there was a TV film crew in the Castle ward at the time, setting up the cameras for a programme. They shot the scene. A flash of it was shown in the local news programme that evening. In Windsor itself everyone knew about it, from the cast of the Theatre Royal performing the latest pre-London thriller to the choir-boys at St George's Chapel.

Anny was told that the police were considering bringing a charge, since violence inside a royal castle counted for something more than a family quarrel. Perhaps it was only a

15

threat, meant to chasten, but Kate and Harry had not waited. They had taken off in Kate's car and not been seen since.

But the interesting thing about the whole episode was that both those who had witnessed the scene and those who had only heard about it, like Anny, were convinced that Kate meant what she said.

She would kill Harry.

Only Charmian remained on the sidelines, wondering what it was all about.

'Has Kate always come on so strong?'

Anny shrugged. 'I don't say she was an easy child. And I know she thought I gave too much time to my work, my own life. I was just beginning, I had to, and anyway,' Anny threw her hands out in a beseeching gesture, 'I couldn't help myself. I was kind of driven. But she knew Jack and I loved her. I thought that would be enough.'

'She was a beautiful baby,' said Charmian.

'But she grew up.'

'I wish I'd seen more of her; I haven't been much good to her as a godmother.'

'You might be getting your chance now.'

Charmian accepted the reference to herself as a police-woman. 'I'll do what I can.'

'She might accept help from you, and I certainly will.' She added: 'And so will Jack.'

'Where is Jack?'

It was always a mystery what Jack did with his day. With his life, really.

'Walking the streets looking for her. A wonderfully wasteful way of passing the time.' It said something about their relationship that Anny's tone was amused rather than censorious.

'You don't really think Kate will kill Harry?'

'Yes,' said Anny shortly. 'I do think.' Then she sat down and momentarily covered her face with her hands. 'No, no, of course not. She is my darling child and I cannot think she will

16

kill anyone. But I do fear something violent and terrible happening.' Her eyes met Charmian's with fear. 'I think he may kill Kate. I'm sure he is violent with her. I saw bruises on her arms.'

'Did you ask about them?'

'She said it was an accident, that she slipped. I didn't believe it. The bruises were wrong.'

'Any marks on him? Bruises? Scratches?'

'None I've seen.'

'She might have been telling the truth then.'

'You know he made her go to a blood donor session and watch him give blood. I didn't like that somehow.'

'We ought to find them,' said Charmian, uneasily. Perhaps Jack had the right idea after all. He often did have good ideas but never seemed to know what to do with them. 'I'll see what I can do. I have a couple of mates in the local outfit.' And there was Humphrey, but he was better left out of it.

'Right,' said Anny gratefully. 'Come and have supper with us tonight and help me calm Jack down.'

But Charmian refused. 'I won't, thanks, love, I've got to work.' She had things to attend to and wanted to get on with them. Work had to be pushed forward. She wasn't here on a holiday, even if it felt like one sometimes.

'I saw a bowl of yours today, Anny,' she said. 'Early red period, I thought. A real beauty. One of your best.'

At last she had raised a smile. 'I know where that was. Molly's been a good customer. She knows what she's buying, too.'

'It's being a success, then, this outfit in Wellington Yard?'

Anny nodded. 'Yes. I get a lot of people dropping in. Sometimes just tourists but sometimes serious buyers. And I've had good publicity locally. I took a stall at the Windsor Horse Show. Very good spot near the Harrods tent and opposite Garrards. I'm doing the same at the Fair in the Great Park. Of course you pay for it.'

Then she added thoughtfully, 'In fact the whole thing costs me an arm and a leg.'

17

Charmian turned to go. She hated that phrase.

There were historical reasons, to do with a bomb, why she disliked it. 'Don't say it,' she said briefly. 'I once saw someone without an arm and a leg. It wasn't nice.'

Charmian walked up the two flights of stairs to her own rooms: a large sitting-room overlooking the Yard, bedroom with the bathroom leading off it, and a tiny kitchen.

Muff leapt at her, demanding attention, food and then freedom in a loud persuasive voice. Charmian gave her the food, a dish of her favourite hard tack in the form of little fish-shaped biscuits. Muff bit into them crisply and neatly, then requested more.

'No, you greedy creature. They swell up inside you if you give them time. Have a good drink of water.'

Rebuffed, the cat took up a position against the door with a view to escaping as soon as it was opened.

Charmian ignored her; she knew a trick worth two of that. 'I'll deal with you, madam, when I go out.' She would be going out. She was always amused how accurately Muff read her intentions. She signalled it somehow. Probably something in the way she moved around the room.

She took off her dress and hung it carefully on a padded hanger, then changed her shoes for soft, easy-to-walk-in flatties, fortunately very fashionable as well this year. The person she was going to see judged you by what you wore. Then she put on a cotton skirt and loose jacket in a cloudy coral shade. With her red hair it should not have suited her, but it did. Then she tucked her notebook in her big shoulder-bag and looked around the room, checking. She did this automatically before she went out so that she'd know if anything was disturbed when she came back. It never had been so far. Why should it? She was just an innocent student doing research.

''Bye, Muff. Look after yourself. I'm off to work.'

She worked in various places and at different hours of the

day, no set routine, round the clock if she felt the need, certainly odd hours. Sometimes she was to be found in the library of the university, and she had a ticket to read in the British Library, but today her work was taking her in a different direction. A lot of her research involved talking to people and asking questions. She was going to meet someone now.

Gently removing Muff's fat body and placing it on a chair, she was out of the door with speed, just beating Muff to the exit by a whisker.

Then she ran down the stairs.

Anny and Jack were sitting at supper, but Anny could see through the window. She paused in a mouthful of chicken casserole.

'There she goes. She thinks I don't know she's up to something but I do. I know her.'

Charmian had caught a glimpse of Anny and Jack as she sped down the stairs and across the yard. Something in their closeness and the way Jack had his arm on Anny's shoulder made her envy them. Jack was a bastard in many ways, idle even if not exactly lazy, living on Anny's money. Passing his days writing music that no one ever performed for films that never got made, he was a loving if ineffectual husband and parent. But their relationship held together, the strands sometimes worn thin, sometimes thorny, full of the prick of past quarrels, but they never broke.

Clever Anny.

She's still a human being, thought Charmian, and I am not.

I have succeeded at my job, but the price that I have to pay is that I am a little separated from my kind.

It made for a kind of loneliness.

The Yard was not a place to be lonely in, however, so it might provide her with a starting point to rejoin the human race. Although evening was coming on, there was plenty of activity.

Charmian could see Jerome and his assistant Elspeth at work on a display of Anny's pots in his window. Jerome admired

Anny's work, and had two huge pots of hers, full of green things growing, at his shop door. After only two weeks and one day in Wellington Yard as a resident she knew how it depended on Jerome. He was so practical. If a fuse went, Jerome fixed it; if a drain blocked, Jerome unblocked it. If you had to get somewhere in a hurry unexpectedly, then Jerome acted as taxi. All this as well as running his own business and looking after his small son. Whether he was a widower or divorced, Charmian did not know and Anny had not said. Be a rash wife who got rid of Jerome, Charmian felt, he was so useful. Dear little Elspeth was his perfect assistant who never seemed to mind odd hours, who looked after the baby when he was busy and was always cheerful. Elspeth had a slim body with a tiny waist and more of a bosom than you would have expected given her other measurements. She seemed mildly proud of this attribute. From Anny who had it from Jerome, she knew that Elspeth's husband was a sailor on the North Sea oil-rig run, ferrying supplies, and that she worked because she was lonely. He was looking for a land-based job and then she would give up work.

She gave a wave to Jerome and Elspeth and got a wave back. The baker's shop and the dairy looked quiet and dark but she knew from experience that there was probably work going on behind the shutters. In the early morning she would smell new bread.

A quick turn right into Peascod Street, then another quick turn and she was passing the Robertsons' shop where she bought her newspapers. They also sold chocolates and cigarettes and she remembered that the person she was visiting liked a present.

Mr and Mrs Robertson were both in the shop. So was Infant Robertson, some few months, sex unknown to Charmian, asleep in a pram. Also, in the back shop, sitting round a table eating high tea were Lindy, Alec, Peter and Essie, the four other little Robertsons. She had heard tell that there were other Robertsons, older and little seen.

Charmian explained what she wanted. 'Do you know those

cigarettes packed in coloured papers, blue, mauve, pink and red?'

These had been Baby's favourites. 'My smokes,' she had called them.

'Are they a bit scented?' Bessie Robertson was plump, and pretty in spite of her family responsibilities which seemed to weigh lightly upon her shoulders. Her husband always looked more worried, no doubt with reason.

'I remember them. Haven't seen them around for a long time. Oh, four years or so.'

Baby had been away for about that length of time.

'Might be some under the counter. When we took over the shop there was a great box of stuff we left alone.' She bent down, ignoring her husband's advice to 'Leave it, Bessie' and presently came up with a dusty box. 'What about these?' On the dented packet was a picture of a Turkish beauty, full length on a couch and wreathed around in clouds of smoke. *Scented Dreams*', said a golden band of lettering above her head. 'Bit stale, eh?' Bessie blew some dust off.

'Better not,' said Charmian. 'I'll take a box of chocolates.' Baby liked chocolates. 'And an evening paper.'

As she paid for her purchases the child woke up and gave a soft wail. 'All right down there?' she asked.

'I don't think he's too well,' said Bessie. 'Just his teeth, I dare say. Our doc's away on holiday, though.'

At least Charmian knew the child's sex now.

'Other doctors,' muttered the father from behind his wife.

'I like our Dr Cook,' she said firmly. 'Your paper,' she said to Charmian who glanced quickly at the newspaper as she walked the few yards to the Zeppo Cocktail Bar where she had arranged to meet Baby.

'A third missing infant found safe,' she read. A third infant? Returned safely, though. It sounded like an interesting story.

She thought about it as she waited for Baby who was late. Probably on purpose. Beryl Andrea Barker belonged to an age

21

and a style that thought you owed it to yourself to keep people waiting.

Baby came up behind her and placed a cool fragrant finger on Charmian's neck. 'Hi. Don't jump, it's only me.'

'I haven't. And I know.'

'Oh I've made you mad,' said Baby with delight. She slid on to the seat opposite Charmian, looking around her with pleasure as she did so. 'Oh I do love this place. Just suits me. What did I do before it was invented?' She was a slender, delicately boned woman built on a core of steel. Even Charmian, who had known her for some time, through various vicissitudes, and knew that she had been a hairdresser, respected the way she kept her appearance together. Her pale silver-blonde hair was lightly tipped with a pinky gold which made a delicate halo round her head. A light sheen on her eyelids matched the gloss on her cheeks, while her lipstick was a soft browny pink that Charmian only wished she could find for herself.

She pushed the box of chocolates across the table. 'I brought you these. Tried to get you some of those cigarettes you used to smoke.'

'I've given them up,' said Baby virtuously. 'You ought to know that. Bad for the skin. At my age you can't afford to run risks. I'll have a Zinzy-Zeppo cocktail, please. That's my special at the moment. They put peach juice in the vodka with a little extra something they won't tell.'

'I wish I could find a lipstick that colour,' said Charmian as she ordered the drink. 'Where did you get it?'

'It wouldn't look like that on you,' said Baby at once. 'It's the chemistry.'

'Oh come on, Baby. I'm not made of different things.'

'I don't call myself that any more,' said Baby, as she grabbed her drink. 'You can call me Andrea. And you are different: more acid.' The cocktail was pale pink with a hint of green in its depths. Baby was enjoying it in neat little sips. The liquid was disappearing quite fast, though.

'Come on then, sweet-skinned, non-smoking Andrea. Work.'

22

Charmian laid her notebook open on the table in front of them.

'Oh dear. I hate talking about *them*. I feel so disloyal. Why can't you get it all from books?'

'Because that's not what research is all about. I do use books. I work in libraries, but I need to ask you questions too.'

'Promise me that it's for the good of them all. I've got my loyalties and memories, don't forget.'

Charmian took a deep breath. 'I promise.' She had in front of her a list of six names:

> Rebecca Amos
> Betty Dedman
> Laraine Finch
> Elsie Hogan
> Nix Hooper
> Yvonne King.

She studied them. 'Really called Nix, is she?'

'I don't suppose she was christened it, but it was what she preferred.'

'And you knew them all pretty well?'

'Yes. And they were kind to me. I wouldn't have got on very well inside if it hadn't been for them. Not a girl like me.'

'Call them friends, would you?'

'I've told you. Yes,' said Baby.

'In all that lot, all of them equal, all the same? Any leader?'

'No, not the same. Not all equal, though. A leader? It has to be Laraine.'

Charmian studied the addresses. Slough, Datchet, Hounslow and Old Windsor.

'Not far away, are they?'

'No. Surprising, really, that we're all so close.'

Charmian smiled. 'Yes, isn't it?'

She was late home, another meeting after Baby.

The Yard was dark.

There was a row of dustbins ready to be emptied. And, resting by them, a black plastic sack.

23

Chapter Three

Charmian woke early and made a large mug of coffee to take back to bed. Muff came in with her, delighted to have company at this hour in the morning. She settled down on the bed purring heavily. After a while she began to make soft but pointed suggestions about food. Charmian ignored her; she was not hungry herself. Muff turned the volume up.

'No, Muff. I've got to drink this coffee while I think.'

Last night, after leaving Baby, she had gone to meet her local partner, a discreetly important police officer, at his home in Old Windsor. He was to be her liaison in the district. Her base was now London, where they had met once before in Humphrey Kent's office. Then he had seemed slightly ill at ease but here, on his own ground, he was relaxed, even cheerful.

He had fed her on beef sandwiches and beer because that was what he was taking himself. 'Wife's away. Made the sandwiches myself. Mustard?'

He had probably sent his wife off on purpose. Most policemen kept their wives out of things. There was a child, too. Charmian had seen a small bike in the hall.

While he ate, he was reading her notes. 'Before you go I'll make a photocopy of all this. OK?' Charmian nodded. He chewed on a piece of beef. 'These women, you think your friend is telling you the truth about them?'

'As she knows it.' Charmian was cautious. In her experience, Baby always knew a bit more than she told.

'This is good work.' He rested a huge hand on her report. He was a large man with a crest of fair hair set above a square face lit by pale blue eyes: a real Saxon. He had the right name, Harold English. She could imagine him at the Battle of Hastings, wielding an axe. And dying. She wasn't sure he liked her, but he was a man whose respect was worth having. 'And you've met them all?'

'Once as a group.' Baby had arranged a meeting in London. 'And then watched them once.' Without them knowing, or so she hoped. She had observed them all together in a wine bar in Eton High Street. 'I hope to be talking to each of them as much as I need. I have to get their confidence.' And, of course, Baby was telling her plenty. She knew how to read between the lines with Baby. 'I have this picture of them. Taken when they all went on a day trip to Dieppe.'

Harold English studied it. 'Look ordinary enough. But they must have something special to have their records. Oh, they're a set all right.'

Charmian appraised the word. Yes, they were a set. You didn't use the word gang of women much, but they could be called so. 'I am specially interested in this one.' She pointed at Laraine. 'And this one.' Nix. You had to be a someone to call yourself nothing.

They continued talking quietly, two professionals discussing their work. Windsor had special problems, he said, with the Castle and all the tourists it attracted. But he could not accept Charmian's view that crime was neutral, no, there were some crimes for women and some for men. They fell into categories. Naturally.

For instance, they had had a series of babies being taken, then returned in a few days, unharmed. Puzzling. But a woman's crime.

'Men like babies, too,' Charmian reminded him. 'Probably desire them passionately sometimes, as much as women.' There was even a movement starting, so she had heard, to research into men bearing the children, nourishing the foetus inside them through the stomach wall.

'Ah,' he looked gently triumphant. 'But some things are special. So happens that one of the babies had a few tests done on it, because it had been sick. The doctor worked out the kid had been breast-fed. Anyway, with human milk. And

25

that's still something a man can't do.'

'So you look for a woman who has recently had a child. And probably lost it. Still-born or a cot death.'

'Yes. Only we can't locate such a suspect.' He gave her a wry grin. 'The field is empty. All such local women seem in the clear.'

She allowed herself ten minutes in which to get round to asking about Harry and Kate; and made it in five.

'Heard about it,' he admitted. 'Nothing to do with me, of course.'

'You're not looking for them?'

'I shouldn't think so. Are you worried?'

He did not ask her why the personal interest, she noticed, he knew.

'I'd like to know.' Then she said: 'And I'd like to know if he has a record.'

'Ah.' Harold English considered, putting his hands on his knees in what she was coming to recognise as a characteristic gesture. 'See what I can do.'

She had got as much as she could for the moment, and because she guessed he liked pretty manners in a woman police officer, she said thank you nicely.

Charmian lay back against her pillows, drinking her coffee while thinking about all this. About Harry who might have a record, and Kate who was a wild one, and Baby who might or might not be leading her up the garden path.

No, she did not think so. Within the bounds of what you could expect from her then, Baby was telling the facts. Baby had changed, after all, desired now to be a respectable member of society called Beryl Andrea Barker.

She stroked Muff's head and the cat murmured something soft about breakfast. Charmian got up and started to dress. A day for a shirt and jeans, but the shirt could be silk and as well made as she could afford. She bought expensive shirts in a shop off Knightsbridge and washed them herself. She had come a long way from the gauche girl who had joined the Force in

26

Deerham Hills, married, made a bit of a mistake of it, but had kept her life going.

What a strange person I've turned out to be, she thought, not what I expected when I left Dundee University with a good degree and no plans for the future except success.

She did her hair and was applying lipstick with a brush when she heard the screaming.

She went to the window and looked down on the Yard. Anny was standing by the dustbins with the plastic sack at her feet.

It was Anny screaming.

She had given two sharp screams, and now was silent. But still standing there, her eyes on the sack. As Charmian looked, Jack appeared at their door and hurried over to Anny. She turned to him and buried her head in his shoulder.

Charmian ran down the stairs and out into the yard. 'What is it? Anny, what's up? Why were you screaming?'

Jack turned a puzzled face to Charmian. 'I dunno. Can't get her to say anything.'

'The sack,' muttered Anny, not looking up. 'In the sack.'

Charmian walked over, dragged open the sack – it was heavier than she'd expected – and looked inside. The smell that rose up at her alerted her to what she was going to find. Flesh. Dead flesh of some sort. A butcher's throw-outs perhaps? But they were nearly all vegetarians in the Yard. Who went to the butcher's? Then she took in what she was really seeing. The gorge rose in her throat. 'God!'

She closed the sack and stepped back.

'What is it?' Jack was still holding Anny in his arms.

'It's a leg,' said Charmian. 'Could be two legs. Or maybe an arm and a leg. I didn't look very closely.' She felt sick.

Anny spoke in tiny little gasps, as if fear was clutching at her windpipe. 'It's Harry. Bits of him. Kate said she'd send them.'

Charmian could see Jerome coming towards them across the Yard, and Elspeth wheeling her bicycle round the corner.

'Get Anny into the house,' she ordered Jack. 'And stop her talking.'

27

Jerome and Elspeth reached her simultaneously. 'What is it?' said Jerome.

Charmian did not answer him directly, she was occupied in stopping Elspeth looking in the sack. She thought Elspeth might be a fainter and a screamer: she felt like being one herself as she held Elspeth's arm.

'Don't look in there. I shouldn't if I were you.'

But Jerome had looked already; he stood back with a grim face. 'Go inside, Elspeth.'

With a frightened face, Elspeth obeyed, disappearing with her bike round the side of his shop.

'The police?' he queried.

Charmian nodded. 'Have to be.'

'You or me?'

'I'll do it.' I like this man, she thought. He accepts what has to be done without arguing. 'You stay here.'

Jerome nodded. 'Give a minute to Elspeth after that, will you? She looks as if she's had a shock.'

Shocks all round, thought Charmian, maybe more than you know.

She made a short call to the local station, heard an explosive sound at the other end, said: 'It's not funny,' and put the receiver down.

Then she went to see Anny. She found her with Jack in their kitchen, where he was dabbing at her face with a towel. 'She's better now.'

Anny moaned. She didn't look better, to Charmian's eye she looked terrible. And there was Elspeth to think about.

'Who's your doctor?'

'Dr Cook, his surgery's just around the corner in York Square. But he's on holiday with his girlfriend,' said Jack, still concentrating on his wife.

'I don't want to know about his sex life, he's got a locum, hasn't he? What's the number?'

Then she felt sorry for Jack, who always got the thin end, who loved his child and must feel bad, too. She touched his

28

arm. 'You make the call, I'll look after Anny.'

Jack turned a dazed stare on her, then stumbled out of the room; she guessed he would have a swift drink before calling the doctor, and for once she did not blame him.

'Anny.' She moved Anny gently to look at her. 'Anny, don't go shouting off about what you think is in the sack. You could be wrong.' Anny gave a convulsive shudder. 'Yes, I know, but still don't say anything. You aren't doing any good. Let the police make their own discoveries.' They will, she thought.

'Where's Jack?'

'Gone to make a telephone call for me. Stay where you are, he's all right. Anny . . . what were you doing out there? And why the hell did you look in the sack?'

'Wanted to put something in the bin.' She paused. 'I could see . . . I know about shapes, I thought I saw a foot.' She looked away. 'I was right, wasn't I?'

'Possibly.'

'You've got your official face on. I haven't seen it often but I know it when I see it. Don't be like that.'

'Well, yes, I think it was a foot.'

'Kate meant me to find it.'

'I think you'd better stop talking like this, Anny.' What kind of a child did Anny think she had bred? What kind of a child had she?

Jack reappeared, amidst a strong whiff of whisky, to give a nod. 'Doc's on the way.' He added briefly and quietly: 'The police have arrived.'

Hard on his heels hurried the doctor, a delightful young woman with a crop of red-gold curls, staggering under the weight of her bag. She was the locum, she announced breathlessly, Dr Cook was due back last night but she was still here, she was going to see Mrs Elspeth Green when she had done here and what was the trouble?

But she proved both efficient and kindly; as Charmian left, she heard her recommending bed and a rest. Probably her standard advice that Elspeth would get as well when her turn came.

Back in her own place she picked up Muff while she stood looking out of the window. Yes, there were the police.

She saw the small group that must include the scene of the crime officer. The man kneeling by the sack was probably the police surgeon while behind him stood a photographer. At the entrance to Wellington Yard two uniformed constables, one a woman, were stationed to keep back onlookers. The dustmen had arrived to be argued with and halted.

It was strange to be on the outside. Yet emotionally she was involved all right. She was in an odd position, one where she could certainly pull rank to find out what was going on, but also one where she must not compromise her other work.

Damn Kate.

No, she must not say that, not even lightly, because Kate might be damned already.

As she stood there, hugging a soft purring cat for comfort, she wondered that Anny had not had the worst thought of all about what was in the sack.

In the Robertsons' shop the news arrived with the dustmen who came in for fags and to pass on the tale. When you knew something like that, then you longed to tell.

A rumour had already reached Bessie Robertson. 'So not a whole dead body then?' she said, a shade disappointed, even in her niceness.

'Bits.' The police constable had not been totally discreet since the man on the bins was a neighbour.

'Could be from the hospital then.' Bessie had a vague notion of spare limbs and organs that the surgeons had done with being put out in the rubbish. Not nice but you could understand it and best not to think about it.

The bin man assured her that it did not work like that and that hospitals had their own ways of disposing of such oddments. He picked up his cigarettes and left. He was for foul play, he said.

30

'What's foul play, Mum?' asked her middle son, Peter, as if he did not know. 'Is it like in football?'

'You shouldn't have been listening.'

He might have said, But I always listen, except that he knew it and she knew it. 'Is it murder then?'

'I wish I hadn't kept you away from school with spots,' said his mother. 'If Dr Cook had been here I wouldn't have, he'd have seen you and sent you back to school.'

Her son responded that he wanted to go to school, he was in the school play and needed for rehearsal.

'What kind of a part have you got, son?' asked his father, appearing at the back of the shop with a stack of boxes.

His son considered. 'I'm like a kind of a fairy,' he said, at length.

'A fairy?' Bessie looked at her son. 'What kind of a fairy? What are you called?'

'Mustardseed.' He added: 'It's Shakespeare.'

'I hope they're teaching you to speak properly then.' Bessie was a Londoner and found the Berkshire accent of her son alien.

'Teacher says the way I talk is the way Shakespeare might have talked,' said her son triumphantly.

'Go and take your spots upstairs.' In any contest with him she usually lost. He was their cleverest child so far, but she had hopes of the baby.

The baby gave a soft wail and Elspeth Green, coming in to buy aspirin and a stamp to write to her husband, looked at him with sympathy. She thought that Bessie, what with the demands of the shop and the other children, did not pay him enough attention. 'Someone'll steal you one day, love,' she said.

'The doctor said to take things quietly and have a rest, so Jerome told me to go home,' she told Bessie. 'I'll have some chocolate, too. You need sweetness for shock.'

Bessie thought she did look pale and worried. Pretty, though. 'I never go white with shock myself,' she said enviously. 'Just all red.'

31

'There's plenty of good red blood inside you, girl,' said Brian, giving her an affectionate slap.

Charmian came in soon after this, and she too bought chocolate. Her body sugars needed topping up also, although her pain and exhaustion came from a different quarter than Elspeth's. Women should look after women, and was she doing this?

She had left Anny behind her with Jack, they did not need her, they had each other. The police team was at work in the Yard, soon they would be interviewing the inhabitants. She had cleared her departure with them, they could talk to her later.

She was on her way to meet Laraine. Baby had set up the meeting. She had arranged to meet Laraine in the bar of the Theatre Royal in Windsor where she had discovered you could get a good cup of coffee in privacy and quiet, which was exactly what she wanted.

Laraine was already there and she recognised her at once, even though she could see that Laraine was the sort of per̲on who changed her appearance regularly. Last time her hair had been in a loose bob, now she was wearing a tight jersey turban of bright emerald. Such hair as Charmian could see appeared to have changed colour too. Surely she had not gone grey? Or was it some effort of Baby's? She had once offered to 'tip' Charmian's hair.

Laraine looked up and gave a wave; so the recognition was mutual.

As she sat down, Charmian remembered what Baby had said.

'Laraine's a marvellous person. She should never have been in prison.'

'You mean she wasn't guilty?' Charmian had asked.

'Oh no, she did it all right, but he asked for it, and she's too good for prison.'

There was always a Laraine figure in Baby's life. The last one had initiated an armed robbery as well as murdering a man, but in a funny kind of way Baby's judgement on moral issues was good. Laraine had gone inside each time for fraud, and there was more than a hint that she might be capable of violence.

Charmian got out her notebooks and arranged her tape-recorder. Laraine looked at it alertly.

'Do you mind if I use it?'

Laraine said she did not, provided permission was always asked. She understood what Charmian was doing and approved. There ought to be a study of why some women kept going back to prison.

Take her own case: she kept going back because she kept getting caught. Why did she keep getting caught, when she was brighter than most policemen?

She did not know and, if Charmian could come up with an answer, she would be doing a real service.

Laraine sat back expectantly.

'But why do you keep committing the same offence?'

'For profit. Money. I don't know any other way a woman like me can make a lot of money. I'm not saying there aren't other ways for different sorts of women, but this was the only way open for me.'

So there was Laraine's reason, and in her mind the account had come out right, more profit than loss.

But perhaps there was something else. 'Women need help. You ought to know that. They have to protect themselves, you see it all round you all the time. I read something in the paper yesterday about a siege in a flat: it'll be a man holding a woman prisoner, you'll see. And then today, what did I hear? A body in a sack. Ten to one it'll be some poor cow a man's carved up.'

Yes, there was something more to Laraine than appeared on the surface. Crime was her business, but it was also her weapon. Baby had caught on to that. It was up to Charmian now to find for whom the weapon was sharpened.

The conversation went on between them over the coffee, quiet and low key. Towards the end, Charmian said: 'And what about now?' She knew that Laraine worked part time in a

33

supermarket, and Nix in a dry cleaner's, while one of them worked in a butcher's. The others were not in work.

'Business as usual,' and Laraine gave the answer with a smile.

Make what you like of that, the smile said.

Charmian walked down the hill from the theatre towards the river. The town was now crowded with tourists and shoppers. She wondered where the locals went in high summer. Hid in their houses probably to emerge at dusk when the visitors had gone. Behind her she could hear the last strains of the band of the Irish Guards as the guard changed at the Castle and one unit marched out and the next came in. It was a daily spectacle, meticulously timed. She wondered how many terrorists had watched and planned.

She sat on a bench on Eton bridge, watching the river run underneath. This place had seen a lot of English history. The Tower of London, Hampton Court and Windsor Castle, royal homes and sometimes prisons, were linked by the river Thames. Not far away was Runnymede, and beyond that Staines where the Anglo-Saxons had forded the upper Thames. No wonder William of Normandy had planted his castle where he did.

It was sunny and pleasant on the bridge, but after a while she got up to walk down Eton High Street, passing all the antique shops and the expensive eating places in search of a quiet telephone to make a private call. She found one as the road turned towards Slough. There was a public call box at a leafy corner where the road looked almost rural.

She called Harold English. 'Hello, anything to tell me?'

Cautiously, he said, 'On one front nothing. Go on as planned. Clear? On that other matter, the question you raised, No, the chap does not appear to have a record. But he has been involved in violence. As a victim. Attacked. Twice.'

'That needs thinking about. . . . You've heard what's been found in the Yard?'

He had.

34

'I'm worried. I suppose no identity yet?'

'No, but there is something you ought to know. It's only what I've been told, but I guess reliable.'

'Go on.'

'Two limbs. But two different people. One a man and the other a woman.'

Chapter Four

A black night, one of the blackest, but still a warm bright day for everyone except Charmian. She walked back down Eton High Street enveloped in her own private darkness. One thought in particular obsessed her. The quarrel that Kate and Harry had in the Castle, had it been about another woman? This was the question she was going to have to put to Anny. But tactfully, because Anny did not yet know about the different limbs in the sack, and must not be encouraged to think about them nor draw either of the dreadful conclusions that presented themselves so tellingly to Charmian. A dead Kate or a murdering Kate? Take your choice. She did not want it to be either.

Jerome was walking by the river. He was pushing his small son in a pram, one of the old-fashioned sort that his mother had dug out of her attic for him. He remembered taking walks in it himself. Or he could be imagining it. Memory could play one of its games with you.

He knew his could. For instance, just now, as he pushed the pram by the river he had thought of Lisa at home, ready with their tea.

Not so; she wasn't there, could never be there again. She was dead. He knew that perfectly well, but just fleetingly, his body had forgotten.

Elspeth was lying on her bed, trying to pretend her headache was getting better. However, it was not; if anything, it was worse. She had no sense of darkness, rather the light worried her eyes. She found the light too bright, too intense and had drawn the curtains against it. Even so she could not cut it out completely. She must be fit to go back to work tomorrow, so much to do before her husband came home. A shorter trip than usual, which was nice, but when you had got used to people

36

being absent for a certain length of time then you had to replan things when they weren't. Quite soon now she would give up working for Jerome, because she hoped to have a child of her own to tend, and he could manage beautifully by himself. When she'd started with him, she had seen herself helping with the child, but he did not need her, she soon saw he could do all for himself. A splendid father, everything arranged for, so different from the Robertsons who never seemed to look ahead. She wondered if Bessie Robertson would be glad of her help in the shop? Preferred her own muddle, probably. As she thought about it she drifted off to sleep, and when she woke up, although she still had her set of worries, she felt much better.

Anny and Jack lay on Anny's big double bed side by side. She did not always let Jack sleep there; he had a narrow bed in what Anny called his dressing room and he called his bunkroom and he was often sent off there. Anny needed a lot of sleep and Jack needed a lot of whisky and the two did not always go together. Now Anny had had a strong nip of whisky too. They were both very unhappy.

Molly Oriel had telephoned to offer sympathy. She made the most practical demonstration of this that she could by offering to help Anny with her stall at the forthcoming Fair in Windsor Great Park. 'No, Anny,' she said, loudly and clearly. 'You must not give it up. On no account. I've told any number of people that you will be there and be there you must.' She did not quite go so far as to say that the Queen herself would be there to buy a pot, but she came very close.

It made Anny laugh, which was perhaps what she had intended. For Molly Oriel it was a bright day, darkened only by sadness for her friend, but one of great personal happiness for herself. Life is such a sandwich, she thought.

Charmian found her gloom lifting as she shopped for an evening meal. She was remembering Kate, thinking of the adolescent she had been, bright and eager. The two had not met often enough, Charmian told herself, but the girl she recalled

37

could not have turned into a double murderer of a particularly brutal kind. Surely not? One had to trust people. Trust, she said to herself. This is Anny's child you are talking about. The trouble was she mixed with so many criminous women who seemed capable of anything that it was souring her judgement. She shopped carefully. There is something honest and cheerful about buying steak and green salad and Brie cheese with oatcakes, things might not be so bad after all. One could not, perhaps, be happy, but one could certainly bear to go on.

She was giving dinner to Nix and Baby tonight. Baby – 'Andrea, remember, Andrea' – had not wanted to come, but Charmian persisted.

'I'm in a hurry. I need to see her. You said you'd help.'

'I'm helping. All right I'm helping. I'll bring her.'

But she arrived alone. 'Nix is coming later. She's got a date with a man friend.'

'Ah.' This was of interest to Charmian. She had wondered when that theme would surface. There had to be a man with that lot. 'Someone she met through prison?'

Beryl Andrea Barker, she was all of that tonight, gilded to her waist with jewellery, gave a hoot of laughter. 'You don't meet a man like that in prison.'

'I said through. You do know him then?'

'Seen him.' Apparently that was all she was going to say.

Nix arrived just as Charmian was putting the steak under the grill. 'Thanks for asking me. Kid here said you wanted to talk.'

Andrea looked smug at being called kid. Clearly that was all right even if Baby was not. 'Had a nice time?' she asked.

'Not bad. Is that garlic on the steak?'

Charmian nodded. 'Do you mind?'

'No, love it. Keeps the bloodsuckers away, did you know? Wonder if it'd do the same for the fuzz?'

Kid, formerly Baby, aiming to be Andrea, said: 'Now that's no talk. You've put all that behind you, Nix.'

'Who said?' She picked out a radish from the salad bowl. 'Well, maybe.'

'I'm fuzz myself,' Charmian reminded her.

'No?' Nix started backwards in pretend horror. 'Now she tells me.' Then she relaxed with a real laugh. 'Yes, I know. Andrea said so. But she says you're genuine.'

Over dinner they talked freely about the sort of thing any trio of women might talk about: clothes, food and, with restraint on Charmian's side and none whatever on Nix's, about sex. Charmian tried to be the one that steered the conversation but she was uneasily aware that Nix knew this and was amused. Come to think of it, with her record she must have plenty of experience in police interrogation and have invented her own ways of dealing with it. But I've had experience too, Charmian told herself, so watch out, my lady.

After dinner, rightly assessing her Nix, Charmian produced a bottle of malt whisky which they drank neat. Over the years Charmian had developed a hard head herself but Nix matched her, drink for drink.

'You got a hollow leg or something?' growled Baby, forgetting she was the ladylike Andrea and picking up her racier persona. 'You'll be pissed.'

Nix just laughed. 'We could finish this bottle.' She held it up to measure what was left. 'Never had a good drink out of a policeman before.'

'Nor a good anything else,' said Baby, still in residence. 'If all you've been saying is true.'

'Perhaps women police are different,' said Nix, leaning across the table and gripping Charmian's wrist with her long fingers.

'Not this one.' Charmian extricated herself coolly.

'I'm ambidextrous, you know,' said Nix with a smile. She held up her left hand mockingly.

'That must have been very useful to you in your career.'

Nix laughed. 'I like you. Be a pleasure to be nicked by you.'

'I hope it won't come to that. . . . Although you do seem to go in and out.'

'And that's what you want to talk about?' Nix's voice sounded light and lively. Almost too lively.

I wonder if she's high on something as well as drink, Charmian thought. 'Do you mind if I make notes?' she asked, trying to drag her down. She produced notebooks and pencils.

'Fire away.' Nix was still airy. 'Just don't tape me; I can't stand the sound of my own voice.'

'I would never have known it.'

'Not taped and on record and ready to bear witness against me at the wrong moment.'

'Tell me the right moment,' said Baby sourly. She was finding it hard to keep up as Andrea, obviously practice was needed.

Nix turned to her. 'You go home, kid. You're tired.'

Baby stood up obediently, as if she had got her cue and must take it. She made polite noises to Charmian and was off.

'She's a child,' said Nix, as soon as the door closed on her.

'You think so?' Charmian asked. It did not happen to be her own opinion of Baby.

Nix put her elbows on the table and looked bright. 'Now to business. Do I just talk or do you ask questions?'

Not high on drugs, Charmian thought, not even drunk. Just high on herself. She's got the confidence of Old Nick.

'We'll start with me asking questions.' She had a list of questions which she was putting to all her subjects. She had drawn them up with the aid of a police psychologist who had also told her what to look out for.

'They'll lie, of course. No matter how much they swear to tell the truth and even believe they can, they will lie. We all do it, and this lot more than most. It's self-protection. Only saints can tell the truth about themselves and even they find it painful.'

'I'm quite good at spotting a lie myself.'

'Of course. But this time you've got to spot the lie behind the lie.'

True, Charmian thought. So I have, dammit, because this is a job within a job. Will I do it? More important, will I do it in time?

Time was beginning to worry her. There was always such pressure in police work, but usually you could show it. Now she must not, but hold it tight inside herself like a secret. Worry over Anny and Kate was not helping her. All the time, at the back of her mind, she was thinking: Whose bodies have we got bits of? And where are the rest of those bodies?

But she controlled herself and talked gently to Nix, not looking for the involuntary change of voice, the eyelid twitch, or the sudden foot movement, for with Nix they would not be there. Instead, as with Laraine, she would look for the fluent patter, the smile at the back of the eyes, the mannered quietness. Nix would have them all, know how to use them, a natural liar if ever she saw one.

And I'm not bad myself, thought Charmian, it takes one to know one.

She went through her questions, asking about family background, upbringing and education, the standard sort of thing. Nix seemed to have no complaints about her family or her school except that they were 'dull' and it had all seemed 'bloody pointless'. Her mother? Oh, Mum had been all right, never had much of a life. Dead now. Dad? Oh, he was still around.

A note in the voice there, Charmian thought. A strong relationship with the mother? Or dislike of the father?

The next questions were about her string of offences. They were a mixed bag from shoplifting to housebreaking, Nix seemed willing to have a go at anything, and this fitted in with what Charmian was beginning to feel about her. Then she started on carefully phrased questions about her friends. The special little group of fellow women recidivists who seemed to be hanging together.

Nix wouldn't say much about them.

Charmian put a question or two about men, Nix's current relationships, if any, but she was not surprised when Nix refused to be drawn.

By certain answers Charmian put a star. Her victim noticed. 'Why are you doing that?'

'They are of interest.' Where I think you have lied, she might have said.

41

Nix stared at the questions as if trying to read them upside down.

'They're in shorthand,' said Charmian, not without sympathy. 'You can't read them. But I'll tell you, if you like.'

'Don't bother.'

'I'll tell you, anyway.'

Nix shrugged.

'The questions where I asked about your group of friends, and asked how you all happened to end up so close now you were out. And you said it was happenstance.'

'Coincidence, I said.'

'Was that the word?' Charmian pretended to study her notes. 'And before that we had agreed it was lucky.' Their eyes met, then Nix looked away. 'And I haven't quite fathomed' – good word, Charmian thought, suggesting depths that she knew must be there – 'I haven't quite fathomed why you do these things because you haven't quite answered.'

'Because you haven't quite asked. I do it for the hell of it. For the kicks. It isn't dull. It makes me feel alive.'

Excitement for Nix and profit for Laraine, Charmian thought, what a dangerous combination they made.

'And is that all?'

'You have to believe in something,' said Nix slowly, 'and sometimes you have to show it. Stand up and say so.' Then she stopped, as if she had said enough.

When Nix had gone, shortly after finishing what was left of the whisky and in the mood to be affectionate and friendly, Charmian went downstairs to ask Anny if she could use the telephone.

Anny, still up and sleepless but in a dressing gown, nodded. 'But use the one in the office. I don't want to disturb Jack. Just got him off to sleep, the great baby.' She sounded weary but calmer. 'Any news?' Charmian shook her head, not prepared to tell her that there had been a part of a woman's body in the sack. 'None here either.' She moved through into the kitchen.

'I'm going to make some cocoa, come in and have some when you're through.'

Charmian spoke to Harold English. 'They are certainly up to something. I can see all the signs, but I can't say more yet. I think it would be worth checking on the man.' Baby had reluctantly supplied a few details and these Charmian passed on: thirtyish, well spoken, a smart dresser, probably had form. A Londoner. 'That's for you to do. But I'm beginning to break through with them.'

She felt half pleased, half a heel. Women should help women. Well, in her way she was trying.

She remembered what Nix had said as she left. 'It's not easy to be a woman like me. Not easy to be a woman unless you've got certain things going for you which I hadn't. You understand me, Charmian, and you'll do some good.'

It was like a wary animal coming forward for a pat.

By midnight all in the Yard were asleep, even Jerome, anxious about his son who had seemed restless. 'Misses his mother,' he told himself. 'Bound to.' Unlike Jack he could not soothe his sorrows with whisky nor with hot milk as could Anny, but he had devised his own means to assuage his grief. You didn't hide from what you felt, you did something about it, you worked hard, you looked after your son, made a success of your business and did something. That way you felt better.

Anny and Jack were not precisely hiding from their anxieties, but they were glad to be asleep and out of the way of themselves for a bit. 'I'll go to the Fair in the Great Park,' Anny told a sleeping Jack as she turned out the light. 'Molly gave me good advice. Of course, Kate's all right. I'll probably hear from her tomorrow and be laughing all over my face.'

Round the corner in the Robertsons' shop the night was disturbed by the baby wailing, and then by the lad Peter asking for a drink of water. 'I itch, Mum, something dreadful.'

His mother examined him. 'It's the spots,' she announced. 'You've got the chicken-pox.' She considered. 'I'll sponge you

43

down. Won't need to bother the doctor now, that's one thing, even if he was back, which he isn't.'

Her son said: 'Mum, there's something I've got to tell you. That night you went to Bingo and Dad was at the British Legion and I was babysitting? Well, I did just go out for a minute, only a minute, Mum, I felt I needed the air.'

'I'll give you air,' said his mother. 'If you didn't have spots I'd give you a smacking for leaving the baby. Well, now you've told me, go to sleep.'

'That's not all, Mum.' Her son gripped her hand. 'I didn't go far, just to see Jerry Gardiner, we had a bet on, and we were where we could see the doctor's.' He paused; his acting experience in *A Midsummer Night's Dream* had not been wasted on him. Then he said: 'There was a black plastic sack on his steps, I could see it plain. And there was a lady standing by it.' He gave an energetic scratch. 'I think it was the sack with the dead body in it.'

Later, in bed, Brian said to his worried wife: 'There's probably nothing in it, you know what boys are, like a bit of drama, especially that one, but you may as well tell the police.'

With all the disturbances, they were late up next day, so that there was more than the usual rush to get the older ones off to work, the rest to school and to give breakfast to the baby and the sick Peter.

At last Mrs Robertson wheeled the baby in his pram to the open shop door where he could get a breath of air and find some amusement from watching the street scene if he wanted. This morning he seemed more inclined to sleep.

Bessie went back inside to the kitchen, poured out two cups of tea and allowed herself the luxury of a sit down while she drank. Her customers were a good lot who would either leave the money for what they owed by the till or give her a shout. 'Where are you?' she called to her husband. 'I've poured you out a cup.'

'Be down. Nearly finished shaving.'

'Take a look at the little 'un as you go past.'

He was a good father and would do just that. The baby was quiet, Peter making no fuss; she enjoyed her cup of tea. A quick glance at one of her magazines would do no harm; she took up a copy of *Woman*.

Her husband came in. 'Where is he then?'

'Who?' She raised her head from her horoscope, which was a good one: *You will have an exciting week in the home.*

'The baby, of course.'

'In the pram.' She stood up, at first surprised but quickly alarmed. 'Isn't he?' She hurried to the pram.

The pram was there, she could see the indentation on the pillow where the child's head had rested. The pillow was still warm when she touched it. But the baby was gone.

Charmian had gone to London very early on the train to Waterloo. There was work to do, checking on the backgrounds of Laraine, Nix and the others. She would be meeting both of them with Rebecca Amos, Betty Dedman, Elsie Hogan and Yvonne King in Windsor tomorrow, or so she hoped. The meeting had been arranged by the reluctantly co-operative Baby. Sorry, Andrea.

She was taking them all to the matinee at the theatre. She understood it was a crime story which ought to be to their taste. They would all sit in a row and be friends.

She did her routine checking, some in Scotland Yard and some on the records in St Catherine's House. She was filling in the details of their lives, trying to see them against their settings. Broken, unsettled homes for the most part, and, for three of the women, Betty Dedman (two brothers inside), Rebecca Amos and Yvonne King, a criminal family. Rebecca's father had been a habitual small criminal, while Yvonne King's husband was a con man of great skill. He was sunning himself in Italy with his current mistress, having long since put Yvonne and his two children behind him. It wasn't true that criminals made good family men, Charmian thought. On the whole they did not.

45

Later that day she went to a meeting in a house so august that she entered it by a back door through the mews.

Humphrey was there, also one other man, whom she had seen once before.

Charmian delivered her report, which was listened to in silence. 'That is as far as I can go at present. I'm sorry.'

'Would it be possible to infiltrate another woman into the group?' asked the Palace official.

'No chance.' Charmian was decisive. 'They are such a strong close group. They only talk to me because of Miss Barker.' And because they think I am honest.

Humphrey said: 'No, you've done well. And we owe a lot to your friend.'

'Yes,' said Charmian, troubled. She wished she could think that Baby was totally disinterested. She wondered what Baby expected out of it. A medal, perhaps.

The last train to Windsor finally delivered her at the Riverside station; fatigued in mind and body, she walked past Alexandra Gardens and under the railway bridge, taking a left turn at the traffic roundabout and then along Peascod Street where she passed the Robertsons'. A young woman was emerging. She recognised her as the doctor, the locum, filling in. The recognition was mutual.

'Hello, met you at Anny Cooper's, didn't I? I've bought one of her pots.' She sounded as tired as Charmian felt.

'Nothing wrong at the Robertsons', is there?'

'Where have you been all day?' asked the girl wearily. 'High drama round here. I don't blame the mother for being hysterical. But it was the boy I came to see now. The worst case of chicken-pox I've ever been privileged to view. I've just had him admitted to the Prince Albert. You missed the ambulance by a second.' In a few more words she let Charmian know about the missing baby, cutting across her reactions. 'And that's not the lot. The boy has some talk about seeing a woman and the black plastic sack outside the doctor's surgery. I've had the police questioning me. They thought it might be me. But it wasn't.'

'No,' said Charmian, realising a response was called for. 'I know nothing about it all. I shouldn't even be here, I've got an exam to take. If only the man I'm filling in for would come back, I'd be off. I don't like this place. Too many strange things happening.' She lugged her heavy bag towards the car. 'I don't like the police breathing down my neck. Perhaps the kid was hallucinating, he does have a fever, but somehow I don't think so. He saw what he says. And it was not me. Isn't that life?'

Life and death, irretrievably mixed up as usual.

Chapter Five

Charmian went straight to her own flat, where she discovered Muff crouching behind the door with her plump form on an unstamped manila envelope which looked at once anonymous and official. The address was typewritten, but there was no stamp, so the letter must have been delivered by hand. From which she deduced that it had come from Harold English. His motives for this kind act would need thinking about. She fed the cat, drank a glass of water, then sat down to read what he had to say.

What she had in front of her was a condensed report of the police investigation on the severed limbs found in Wellington Yard. She was being given a private look behind the scenes. Even as she inwardly thanked English for his courtesy, she was grasping the fact that he thoroughly understood her own emotional involvement. He had done his homework, he knew of her long friendship with Anny Cooper, he had known the gossip about Kate, heard the stories, probably come to a few conclusions of his own. No doubt he knew also what his colleagues thought of it all, although no hint of this came through. It would have been nice if the report could somehow have eliminated Kate from any connection. But it did not.

She took the report with her into the kitchen while she ate her supper of bread and cheese. Muff had eaten rabbit cat food from a tin, her favourite brand. Tomorrow she might fancy something different, Muff had her own ways of letting her mistress know these things, and her own technique for ensuring action. Charmian devoted more time and thought to planning Muff's menu than she did her own.

A crumb of bread fell on the page she was reading. She brushed it away, noticing that it had left a soft buttery stain behind which had highlighted a word: blood.

The limbs had been severed after death with a sharp instrument applied by an unpractised hand. The job had been well done but not elegantly, the blows cutting across bone and muscle with more regard for symmetry than anatomy. Not, then, the work of a surgeon or a butcher. An amateur job. There would have been blood. Plenty of it.

The time of death could only be speculated upon, but decomposition of the limbs was not far advanced. Say some twenty-four hours before the limbs turned up in Wellington Yard. They were working on this.

One leg was that of a man of light build, thin but tall, probably approaching six feet in height. The hairs on the leg were dark, the skin fair.

The other leg had belonged to a plump young woman who had been estimated to be about five feet and four inches tall. A blonde.

There was a light deposit of some as yet unidentified powder on both legs. This was now being studied, and when identified might provide a useful pointer to where the bodies had rested before turning up in Wellington Yard.

There was, as yet, no indication where the rest of the bodies were. Nor why the legs had been cut off, nor why the legs had been deposited in the Yard.

The case was being treated as a major murder enquiry, a double murder of a particularly brutal kind. Missing people were being checked.

No mention, she noted, of the boy's story about seeing a woman near the sack outside Dr Cook's surgery. News of that might have come in after this report was put together. No mention either of Kate and Harry.

So that was it. Charmian was putting the report in a drawer when the front door bell rang. She paused only for a moment before answering it.

'Anny! Welcome, I could do with some company. I'm just going to make some coffee. Like a cup?'

Anny followed her into the kitchen. 'I designed this kitchen, you know.'

'I did know, Anny. It bears all the marks of you.' Also, every piece of china in the apartment had been made by Anny herself, and was unmistakably her work. The very tiles that lined the bathroom were her design: leaping dolphins on a terracotta background.

'Meaning?'

'Comfortable, well designed and good to look at.'

'Thanks.' Anny sat down and reached out for the mug of coffee. The mug was aquamarine blue from her green-blue period which had come after the red period and preceded the yellow which she was in now. 'You're cheering me up, aren't you?' Her tone suggested Charmian might not find it easy.

Still, Charmian noticed that her friend had had the spirit to have her hair newly washed and cut. 'Your hair looks nice.'

'Jerome did it for me this morning.'

'Is there anything that man doesn't do?'

'He used to be a hairdresser, before he took up other things. He's been everything, that man. Go yourself.' Suspiciously, she said: 'You're still cheering me up.'

'If you want something else I can give that, too.' Her eyes went to the drawer containing the report.

Anny's gaze followed hers, not without comprehension. She was as quick at reading body movements as Muff. Her lips tightened.

'I know about the other leg being a girl's leg,' she said. 'Also about the woman seen standing by the plastic sack outside Dr Cook's. Word gets around. Would you call Kate a woman?' she said in an expressionless tone. 'Not really old enough, is she?'

'To a boy perhaps.'

'He's a liar, that boy,' said Anny.

Charmian said nothing. She did not believe he was: there was a ring of truth to the story as she had been told it.

'Don't you think so?' Anny tried again, but without much conviction in her tone.

50

'And you can't go and have it out with him because he's got chicken-pox and the baby's been snatched,' said Charmian with sympathy. 'And you wouldn't go anyway, because you don't really think he's lying. And as it happens he's just been whisked off to hospital.'

'But it might have been a fantasy thing. I knew he was pretty ill. If he had a high fever then, he might have been imagining things.' Anny finished her coffee. 'But Jack doesn't think so. He's had to have a whole bottle of Bell's to stop thinking about it.'

'He'll kill himself.'

'And I don't know what to believe. What do you think, Charmian?'

'Let's put it this way – which would you prefer: that Kate is the killer, or that she is a mutilated corpse?'

It was a brutal but necessary shock to Anny.

She put her hands over her eyes as if to shut out the picture Charmian was so vividly calling up.

Charmian said: 'I think we'd better decide that this affair has nothing to do with Kate and Harry. Right?'

'Right,' said Anny.

For a moment, Charmian thought she had quietened Anny's fear, but Anny was not so easily soothed. With her, at this time, anxiety was pushed out of one door only to come in at another. She had a newspaper in her pocket that she pulled out.

'Do you think that Kate can be the woman held in this house siege in Ealing?' She pointed to the paragraph in the evening paper where there was a picture of the house, a neat bow-windowed villa, with a story saying the police had decided it was 'a domestic affair' and would draw back from confrontation for 'the time being'.

'No.' Charmian was firm, although she had considered this possibility herself. 'But if you want to make sure, go to the house and take a look.'

'I might just do that,' said Anny, with energy. 'That would surprise you.'

51

'No.' Charmian shook her head. 'No more than it would surprise you if I came too.'

Their eyes met, and they began to laugh.

Thank God, thought Charmian, I have broken her mood.

They had been friends for such a long while, and trusted each other and told each other secrets, so that now there was no need for telling, they could read each other well.

Charmian knew that the dreamy drunken Jack suited her friend who would never leave him, but that her strongest emotions were first for her work and then for her child; Jack came third. Still, he was on the list and perhaps that was enough for him or perhaps it never had been and that was why he drank.

Anny knew that there was a hole inside Charmian that needed filling and that if Humphrey did not fill it then someone disastrous would and she was on guard against that person.

One of the things that marked this strange time for Charmian was the way she was split right down the middle.

On the one hand was her developing relationship with the Girls, getting weirder all the time as they treated her as something between a tame cat and a guru.

On the other hand, the way she had settled into the community of the Yard. She liked it so well there that she was even considering whether she could live there permanently when she took up her new job in London. She would be able to joke that she worked in one Yard and lived in another.

If she stayed, she would have to get a telephone put in.

She thought that as she walked into the theatre where she caught sight of herself in a mirror. Jerome had washed and cut her hair that morning, the appointment arranged on Anny's telephone, one didn't just walk in on Jerome; he had done it beautifully but differently, so that it was like looking at a stranger with a familiar face.

She stopped for a minute. No, now she knew what it was. He had brought back that gawky, shy girl with reddish hair who had come down from Scotland to conquer the world.

Anny had put her head round the door as she sat in Jerome's having her hair finger-dried while he talked. 'I tried hair-dressing when my wife died,' he was saying. 'Took a diploma but I decided to change to something where I could stay at home and keep Keith with me. I can turn my hand to most things, done most things too.' He grinned at her. 'Master of none.' Keith was sitting at the table crayoning a picture book. His father looked at him proudly. 'Advanced for his age, isn't he? I don't let anyone do anything for him but me. Elspeth is always offering, but I prefer not. No, she's away today, not sick, getting ready for her husband coming back, I expect. She's a pesky little creature sometimes, but very trustworthy with Keith. Of course, as you can imagine, I'm not letting him out of my sight at the moment, with that poor little Robertson kid going missing.' He moved Charmian's head gently so that he could see the shape he was creating. 'Funny old world, isn't it? Yesterday we had the police all over the place and now it's gone dead quiet.'

But police work was like that, as Charmian very well knew, the appearance of quiet being deceptive because a lot of dull, routine checking would now be taking place from which the truth might, with luck, eventually emerge.

From the door, Anny said: 'Tonight?'

'Tonight,' agreed Charmian.

Jerome raised his eyebrows. 'Going on the town? Blazers is the best night spot round here.' Wouldn't mind taking her there myself: after all, I'm still a man, not only a father; he lowered his eyes, letting his thoughts roll on.

'Just an expedition we're taking,' said Charmian.

Jerome had given his attractive half smile and with a snip of his scissors had lightened her hair and her looks.

Now she smoothed her hair in the big mirror while she looked around for the Gang.

Then she saw Nix and Laraine standing together by the entrance. Nix gave a little wave. 'We're in the bar. Coffee and

53

sandwiches only, because the bar isn't serving anything else, but you may find a little something extra in the cup.'

Following them down the stairs to the bar Charmian allowed herself another mild wonder at the source of Nix's high spirits. Possibly they were self-manufactured again, a natural by-product of her body's metabolism, and if so she was a lucky lady. In Charmian's experience, depression was what women more often got from their body's swings and balances.

Something else to consider was the source of the mild prosperity that suffused the group, from Laraine's smart expensive trouser-suit to Yvonne King staring happily at a pair of new shoes. In her opinion they were getting money from somewhere.

'Hello,' said Baby softly. She had an empty cup by her and on her face a smile that stayed in place. It did not waver as she stood there, although she herself, very faintly, did. Whatever had been mixed with the coffee had been strong. She took a sip of her own and let it rest on her tongue. Brandy, and plenty of it.

Baby took a step backwards and sank down on a banquette of red plush. 'I haven't got a very strong head,' she said modestly.

Charmian sat down beside her, cup in hand.

'I'm frightened,' said Baby in a soft voice.

'Of whom?'

'Of them, of course.' She gave a quick look at the group still at the bar, Nix standing by Laraine, a head and shoulders the taller, with Yvonne King, Rebecca Amos, Betty Dedman and Elsie Hogan slightly apart. As no doubt they felt themselves to be, for Laraine and Nix were certainly the leaders. Between those two there might yet be rivalry, but at the moment all was harmony.

'Your hair is lovely,' said Baby, still keeping her voice down. 'And I ought to know. Takes years off you. Who did it?'

'I had it done this morning. Jerome in the Yard.'

'He did a good job.'

Nix called across from the bar: 'What are you two talking about?'

'Hair,' said Baby. Quickly.

'No secrets now,' and Nix turned back to her band of friends.

'See what I mean?' muttered Baby. 'Checking. Don't blame her, but doing it.'

'Why are you frightened?'

'Because of what they'd do to me if I wasn't loyal.'

'But you are loyal.'

'If I wasn't.'

Charmian considered; she knew what Baby was doing. What she so often did: putting herself in the right position to escape. In her life she had made several escapes from tricky situations. Self-preservation was built into Baby as into a cat. She still had most of her nine lives left.

'I'll look after you,' Charmian said. To herself, she added: If I can.

She got up and went to the bar. Betty, Elsie and Yvonne were standing together. Betty spoke up as she approached, her tone aggressive. She was an aggressive woman, Charmian had noticed it before.

'You're writing a book about us.' Charmian made a demurring noise: not exactly a book, a study. 'I could write a book myself if I wanted. Plenty to say, but I haven't got time. Yvonne here wants to talk to you. She's never been able to write, well, not really. Do her name naturally, but not what you call communicate. Can't read much either, can you, Von? No, it's held her back. She feels she'd have got on a lot better if she'd been able to write. Letters home, that sort of thing. That's it, isn't it, Von?'

'Yes,' said Yvonne, as if speech too was something that she found hard to come by. 'I could write to my children if I knew how to write and if I knew where they are. Could you help me?' She looked down at her shoes, sadly. 'And I don't think these shoes are any too good a fit, either.'

Nix tucked her arm confidently under Charmian's elbow as they trooped in to their seats. 'We've all got lots of questions to ask you. You're going to be so useful to us.' Charmian saw she was quite in earnest. 'Yes, as a woman. You can tell us things. Oh, I don't mean about sex and such, we could probably give you some hints there.' She giggled. 'But about our rights as women, and what we can do to protect ourselves. I don't reckon we've ever had any help on that.'

The sad thing was she was quite right.

By the end of the afternoon the strangeness of the little group and of her place in it was so overwhelming that she felt suffocated. It was a physical thing, which she could not deny. She was both attracted and pushing away at the same time, almost like a love affair that had gone wrong.

Baby was quite right to feel fear. Together, this group was stronger by far than any of its parts, a corporate animal with a power of its own. An animal that at this moment trusted her but might at any time spring forward showing its teeth.

And what was this strange animal about to do? Why had it drawn itself together? To what end and for what purpose? Because it had one, of that she was sure.

Coming out of the theatre, while receiving their thanks for the amusement (Nix's ambiguous word), she made appointments to see Yvonne, and then Betty, Elsie and Rebecca separately in their own places. This was a step forward. You could tell so much from home territory. They were all very territorial animals, these women; part of their criminality rather than their femininity, perhaps. It was interesting, these three women were allowing her in. Nix and Laraine had not. For them, she would have to wait.

'You don't mind me digging?' she asked Nix.

Nix consulted Laraine with her eyes. 'No, we don't mind.'

Which was true, they seemed to be enjoying the digging into their lives.

And that was strange, although in Nix's bold stare and Laraine's pale gaze she read duplicity.

Perhaps she was getting a reflection of her own eyes back.

*   *   *

56

That evening another limb was found in a black plastic sack. This sack was found by a couple of municipal workmen among a heap of rubbish on the town tip on the road towards Slough. The leg inside had belonged to a man.

They reported it to their foreman who at once telephoned the police. Then they sat waiting.

It was raining in Ealing. Charmian sighed for a moment about her freshly arranged hair. 'Am I doing this to satisfy you?' she asked Anny. 'Or are you doing it to satisfy me?'

'Your idea, remember.' Anny had a headscarf and a raincoat on, she had thought about the weather. Or did she just need to be shrouded? It was certainly hard to see her face.

They were standing at the corner of Belvedere Crescent, a row of Edwardian villas which had gone down in the world without starting to rise like some of its neighbours. Charmian felt that the scales had gone too far one way and might never come up again. The demolition gangs and the developers could not be far away. Many of the houses stood in need of redecoration while even those which had received it had been done over in bold, garish colours like cobalt blue and scarlet which ill became their seedy old age. The kerbs were lined with cars, all old, as far as she could see, with no new registrations among them. Her professional eye never failed to register this kind of fact.

'Long time since you've done this kind of police work,' said Anny. She leaned against a wall and took out a packet of cigarettes. 'Can you work out which house it is?'

'It has to be the one the plainclothes man is watching.'

'I don't see him.' Anny was surprised.

'He's the one sitting in the van reading a paper.'

'I thought he was a workman skiving.'

The two women moved quietly down the street to where they could get a better view.

'There's a man in that yellow car,' said Anny.

'He's probably a journalist, hanging around to see if anything breaks.'

'How can you tell?'

'I'm just guessing.' But she knew she was right: you develop a sense on these things.

'Aren't there any real people? No genuine inhabitants around?'

'Not out in the rain.'

But there was an unreality to the street, it felt like a film set to Charmian's sharpened perceptions. Anny had picked up this feeling without recognising it.

Anny said sharply: 'There's someone at the window. I saw the curtain move.'

Charmian had seen it too, a face looking out, then moving back. 'Did you recognise anyone?'

'I can't be sure.' Anny looked worried. 'I don't know. I hardly got a look. It could be Kate.'

'It was a woman then?'

'I think so. Didn't you see?'

Charmian said slowly: 'No. Nothing to identify. Sorry, Anny.'

Anny was determined. 'I'm not giving up.'

A uniformed constable was coming towards them from the corner. He was wearing a raincape and pushing his bike. Charmian was totally unsurprised by his appearance; she had expected someone to turn up. They were watching but they would also be watched.

Anny became aware of his approach at the same time. She waited silently, as he came up.

'Good evening, madam. Is there any trouble? Anything I can do?'

'It's my child,' said Anny. 'I think my daughter is in that house.'

'Have you any reason to think so, madam?' He was a careful young man, and his speech showed it.

Anny was silent.

Charmian intervened: 'Her daughter is missing. We just came to look. Thought we might get a glimpse of a face.'

'A couple in there, but we don't have an identity for them. Squatters. I doubt if it is your daughter.' He was kind and sceptical.

Anny said, 'I'm going to ring the bell.'

'You could ring, madam, but I wouldn't advise it. Our information is that any interference might trigger off trouble. We're letting it simmer.'

This time they all noticed a curtain at an upper window move. This time there was nothing but a hand to see.

'What do you think?' Anny asked as they drove away. 'Is it Kate? Could it be?'

'I don't know what to make of it. No, I think not Kate, if you want my real opinion. I don't know where Kate is.' After a while, Charmian said: 'Does Kate have any friends in Windsor?'

'She hasn't been around much to make any. She has one, a girl she knew at school who is working here, a young doctor. Amanda Rivers.'

'I might try talking to her,' said Charmian. 'Or you could.'

They drove back to Wellington Yard in silence.

'Your poor hair,' said Anny, as they parked.

'Never mind. I can have another session with Jerome.'

And that looked like being the best thing to have come out of the day. Later, sitting in her bath, watched at a safe distance by Muff, Charmian decided she was looking forward to the prospect.

When she emerged from the bath, she found another note from Harold English pushed under the door.

He must have a secret messenger, she decided irritably. Somehow these silent deliveries invaded her privacy.

He wrote: Your group of subjects have a contact. One Joseph Delaney, an Irishman, now living in South London. He has a record. Details attached. He may be an IRA sympathiser, but basically he will do anything for money.

The girls had a light meal at the Pizza Parlour after the theatre

59

and then split up; they seemed to feel no desire to stay together.

Nix scratched herself vigorously as she walked towards the bus stop. 'I hope I haven't got chicken-pox,' she said to Laraine. 'That really would bugger things up.'

Laraine did not answer. In her opinion it would make no difference at all to their plans.

But if anyone got chicken-pox she hoped it was Charmian. It would have amused her.

While all these separate activities had been going on, the police team searching the town tip in the rain came across another limb, once again inside a black plastic sack. This leg belonged to a woman.

Now they had two matching sets.

Chapter Six

The local police, always loaded with plenty of responsibility because of Windsor being what it was, the home of sovereigns, and the second calling place after the Tower of London on every tourist coach trip, now felt they had more than their share.

As usual there were the customary summer cases of cars stolen, tourists robbed, and houses being broken into. A variation this year was the way the luggage was disappearing from parked coaches. They had never had this before and it was causing concern. Locking the coaches seemed to make no difference: the luggage continued to melt away. In addition, they were having trouble with a small group of adolescent glue sniffers who were making a nuisance of themselves. The youngsters congregated in a church on the outskirts of the town where they frightened the old ladies who were in the habit of using a path through the churchyard as a short cut into town. Also there was a long-running investigation into a series of poisonings in an outer estate. The estate was a smart one with expensive houses lived in by bright, up and coming young couples. No one had died, but some people were unpleasantly ill, and the police could not get to the bottom of it. In time they would, because they had a hunch who was behind it, but that was about as much as they could say at the moment. Which did not satisfy the press.

But over and above all these crimes, they had the puzzle of the stolen babies, who were usually gone a couple of days and then returned, as if they had done their job. If babies can be said to have a job. The Robertson baby was still missing and the police were getting worried. His three days were up, and if he was going to come back then it was time he did.

And finally, there was the mystery of the severed limbs found in the sack in Wellington Yard, which they could now match up with the legs found on the rubbish dump. This was a nasty one, giving no pleasure to anyone except the press who were finding it useful at a time of dull news. (Except for the poisonings on the Blossom Hill estate, which had temporarily ceased.) They were pressing the police, who had nothing much to tell them. So far, the heads, arms and trunks of the dismembered man and woman had not been found. With any luck, these would turn up elsewhere and outside their patch, which would mean it was someone else's problem.

Meanwhile the four specimens were giving work to the police pathologists and forensic experts.

It was soon established that all four limbs had been cut off by the same instrument, no doubt by the same hand and probably within the same time period. It was like the brushwork on a painting, you could recognise the style. The cut marks on each leg had the same neat, regular look as if one person had worked away without interruption.

All four limbs had traces of some substance which was discovered to be flour. Straightforward household flour as used in home baking. Under the microscope it looked coarsely ground with its full share of particles of husk.

The laboratory worker who did the analysis knew what he was looking at but did not know Wellington Yard.

The policeman who read the report first knew Wellington Yard, but did not pick up the significance of what he read. He was tired and out of sorts that day, because of a quarrel with his wife.

A miss then.

The link would not, of course, be missed for ever, perhaps not for very long, but for the moment there had been no connection.

But the grouping of the four legs together in a good light did flush up one fact that had not been noticed before: the legs were sun-tanned.

*   *   *

On the Datchet Road stood the Prince Albert Hospital, built in 1886, hit by a bomb in 1941, and totally rebuilt in 1960, when there was still a bit of money around for building. The design had been award-winning, the first major project of a young architect later to win a Gold Medal. He had been proud of his construction, because it was good to look at, the roof did not leak and the windows were in the right place, giving sunlight but no discomfort to the inhabitants who did not feel they were living in a fishbowl. It was a popular, small hospital, constantly under threat of closure because of its size but with plenty of active local support that rallied to its defence when it needed it.

Like the police the Prince Albert came under pressure at this time, since it was missing a consultant and one junior doctor as well as being short of nurses on several wards.

The consultant was away at a conference in Virginia where he was reading a paper; he was passionately envied by his junior colleagues for this outing. They looked forward to the day when it would be their turn. The junior doctor, who worked in obstetrics, had not yet returned from holiday.

The well attended and hard-working paediatric department was particularly feeling the strain because of the chicken-pox epidemic. Such epidemics have their own pattern of appearance in the young population. They are not uncommon or usually serious, but this one was proving nastier than most. Here and there were some very sick children. South Windsor had a pocket of such cases, all of whom were being nursed in the Prince Albert. One of these was young Peter Robertson.

He was in a small side ward and his mother was with him. Parents were encouraged to stay with sick children, anyway, but Bessie Robertson was a special case. She was the mother of both a very ill boy and a missing baby. Under such terrible double stress, Bessie needed attention herself, so since her own doctor was still away, the hospital had taken her under its wing.

It so happened that all the babies that had been lifted had been delivered in this hospital. Whether this was of significance

63

or not had yet to be established, but it was certainly interesting. Practically speaking, it had meant the obstetric and gynaecological department coming under scrutiny from the police, who were in and out all the time, asking questions. They found it hard to believe that the department could not, somehow, lead them to a suitably guilty nursing mother. Some of the doctors, nurses and hospital staff had found this easy to bear, others had not.

So the police had reason to be around the Prince Albert Hospital.

In addition, the boy himself was a witness (if you could believe him) in the severed limbs case. He had seen the first plastic sack at a time and place before it appeared in the Yard, he had seen a woman standing by it. The police wanted to ask him about these statements. They had questioned the boy out with him on that night, but the friend said he had noticed nothing. So it was all up to Peter Robertson, when he could talk. That wouldn't be just yet, the doctors said.

A young policewoman spent a lot of the day with Bessie and Peter, just in case. She was in plain clothes, being on probation for the detective branch. It was an important step for her, an ambitious girl, with a pretty face, good voice and an acute mind.

She was well primed with the questions she would ask if she got the chance. At the moment, mid afternoon on the day after Charmian and Anny had looked for Kate and Harry in Ealing, the Girls had eaten a pizza supper after the theatre, and the two other legs had turned up, Bessie and Peter were asleep, and the policewoman felt drowsy herself. But she was a conscientious girl, so she forced herself awake.

This girl was an admirer of Charmian Daniels, had taken her as her career model, and meant to be equally successful. Although Charmian was keeping herself in the background and saying nothing, she was the object of much quiet observation from the local Force. They might not know what she was up to, but they knew she was there. She was a name, a figure to be

64

watched. She had done things in the past that made her a legend.

For someone like WPC Dolly Barstow she had helped establish the position of women in the CID. Of course, she had not been happy in herself as a person, or so one heard, but Dolly meant to do better. To begin with, she would not marry, or if she did, then her husband would not be a fellow policeman.

A nurse came into the room, took the boy's pulse, then smiled at Dolly.

'How is he?' Dolly had got the present task because she had had chicken-pox, a nasty go, and she knew what it felt like.

'Coming on nicely.'

'He hasn't said much.' Nothing really, just the odd mutter. He seemed to sleep all the time.

'Oh, there's no brain damage.'

'Could there be?'

'Well, you never know.' She smiled again and departed.

Bessie had not stirred. Just as well, Dolly considered, since there was still no news of the baby, if she could sleep the time away – she might wake up one hour and learn he was back. With luck. Quietly, she took herself off in search of a cup of coffee. She had learnt to avoid the coffee of the Prince Albert.

She had not wasted her time at the hospital where she was already on friendly terms with several of the nurses and a few of the doctors. She had eyed one of the senior housemen, who had an air of patrician dreaminess which took her fancy, such a change from her colleagues. Moreover, he liked her. Without a word being passed between them, they had managed to meet several times at the coffee-machine.

The special coffee-machine, of course, in the doctors' common-room, which made real coffee, not the sad coffee in paper mugs which was provided for patients and visitors in the lobby.

She poured her coffee, avoiding sugar and cream. Her training allowed her to take in the room at a glance, without appearing to do so, a very useful trick to a hopeful girl. He was not there.

A hand touched her elbow. She gave a jump. 'Oh, you.' She dabbed at her skirt.

'I walked in behind you. Sorry if I made you spill your coffee on your skirt.'

'It's had worse on it.'

He wasn't quite with her today. Mind on his work, probably. Yes, he was taking a quick look at his watch.

He never talked about his cases. She respected his professionalism, it was how she liked to behave herself. He talked about his colleagues sometimes, but with discreet amusement, as if he was talking about strange animals of a race subtly different from his own. This was the quality that Dolly so liked about him.

A voice from the door hailed him. 'Len?'

Yes, this was his name, the only unstylish thing about him. Dolly never used it, secretly she hoped it was short for something finer. Perhaps it was Lancelot. One wouldn't use Lancelot, she could see that, but it would be there in the background.

The speaker was a tall young woman, another doctor, of whom Dolly was a little jealous. She had noticed that Len did not make jokes about Fiona.

'Can I have a word?' She gave Dolly a brief smile, as if Dolly was not important but could not be ignored.

Len poured himself some coffee, but did not move from his spot near Dolly. 'Speak on.'

'How are you feeling?'

'Well, thank you.'

'Good. Because one by one people are going down with infections. Gervase has chicken-pox.'

'I've had it,' said Len promptly.

'So have I. Of course, I've got migraine and I might have flu, but I can't go sick because everyone else has got in first.'

'Is that what you came to say?'

66

'No, that was just a cry of pain.' And she relapsed into a technical conversation about the advisability of inducing labour in a difficult case, who was making a fuss about natural childbirth.

'I always say: Tell me what you don't want,' said Len, in a practical way. He made one or two suggestions which Fiona accepted.

Dolly thought she looked very tired. In a burst of sympathy she poured some coffee and handed her a cup.

'Oh thanks,' and this time Dolly got a real smile. 'I must dash. I'm covering Amanda Rivers' slab on the rota, and if she doesn't get back soon I shall scream.'

'Not on the ward, I hope. Sister would not stand for it.'

'No, to the Hospital Administrator,' said Fiona grimly, sounding as if she meant it. She drank the coffee, then made for the door.

'I must go too,' said Dolly to Len. She had been away too long as it was.

They eyed each other. A decisive moment was approaching and they both knew it. Either forward or back it must now be. Dolly took the plunge for them both.

'I'm off duty tonight.' She had already recognised that she was probably the keener of the two.

'I'm on call. I could bring my bleeper, though.'

The step had been taken. After all, bringing your bleeper home to a girl is a decided advance towards intimacy.

'Right. I can't say I won't get a phone call myself. You never know in my job.' It was something they had in common.

Together they walked towards the main lobby from which all ground floor corridors radiated. At this time in the afternoon it was quiet and uncrowded. It might at any moment explode into life with an emergency, but for the moment the two young women at the reception desk had time to talk to each other.

'I know why you are here, of course,' said Len. 'Stories have gone around. How is the boy?'

'Not talking.'

67

'It's a funny business.'

'Which one?'

'Mm.' Len acknowledged her point. 'The mysteries in a small town.' Not that you could really call Windsor a small town. Or not the average small town. In size perhaps, but as an idea it was very big. 'You must know what is going on in the investigation on the kidnapped babies.'

And it was not much. 'Yes.' A lovely, pedantic way of putting things he had. As she did not say.

'But you couldn't discuss it.' It was hardly even a query; he took professional silence for granted.

'No.' Although that did not mean she might not, given the right circumstances. 'Why?'

'Just something I've been thinking about.' He looked towards the lifts. On the third floor a patient was waiting for him.

'Want to say?'

'A thought I had. Might be nothing in it. I'll go on thinking about it. Tell you tonight.'

It could do me a lot of good to come up with a really bright lead. As once again she did not say aloud. She knew without being told that although ambitious himself he would not promote hers. Charmian, her model, had taken her first big step forward when a murderer fell in love with her. Or so the story went. This case was quite different, of course. But you did need a bit of luck. Dolly decided to hang on to her luck.

'Tonight it is.' She gave him directions how to find her flat: Middle of the town, you can walk it. Run back to the hospital if you have to. And I'll run with you if I haven't got what I want out of you by then.

One of the women at the reception desk was taking a telephone call, her gaze wandering from the doors to the lifts as she did so.

Charmian pushed open the big swing doors. You're not supposed to get emotionally involved, she told herself.

Behind her was a day in which she had had a session with her supervisor, had spoken to Humphrey Kent about Mr Delaney

68

on the telephone, and had made arrangements to see Yvonne and then Elsie at home tonight.

She was smarting slightly: her supervisor, a middle-aged don, approved of what she had done so far but seemed to view her efforts with the same faint scepticism as her police colleagues. 'You know something I don't know,' his expression had seemed to say, 'but I do not desire to know it. I am a scholar, between us is a gulf fixed.' It was disheartening.

Then he examined her. 'What questions are you asking? Are you asking if women criminals are different from men criminals? Is their criminality of a different type? Do women only fall into crime when they lack a strong family nexus? Should we, indeed, use the word fall? Does it imply a sexist basis in the way we talk about women criminals? Are these the questions you are asking? And what sort of answers do you look for? You know, by the way, the true scholar does not look for the answers, they fall on him from the heavens, he is surprised.' This bit was not disheartening, but it was gruelling.

Now she had taken a few minutes for her own private enquiry.

She looked around, caught the abstracted gaze of the woman on the telephone, and turned towards Dolly and Len. As one actress will recognise another, so she knew Dolly at once for what she was.

'I'm searching for Dr Amanda Rivers. Can you tell me where she is?' The receptionist left her telephone and came across to Dolly. 'I was looking for you. There's a call. That telephone over there.'

Dolly went across to take the call. She listened, did not say much in reply, then came back with a sober face. 'It's the missing baby. I have to tell Mrs Robertson.'

So Dolly Barstow, apprentice police detective, went off to see Mrs Robertson; Dr Len Lennard, first name Aylwin, departed to help his patient to deliver her child; and Charmian Daniels, denied a meeting with Amanda Rivers, but having obtained her home address, had set off for Wellington Yard.

69

Laraine, Nix, Betty, Rebecca, Yvonne and Elsie had each finished their day's business and gone to their own places without communicating with each other that day. Nix, whose antennae were sensitive, had picked out from the air the sense of hostile observation. It was a general feeling she had, one she did not pin on Charmian specifically, but it was hanging over her head and might at any moment settle on her.

Len was thinking about his patient, but also about the babies and the way they were fed; he had an idea.

Dolly was thinking about the Robertson baby but also about Charmian, whom she had identified accurately.

Charmian was thinking about Kate and the women whom she thought of variously as the Girls, the Group or the Gang.

They were thinking only of themselves, and what they had in store for life. Well, perhaps not the whole of life, this little bit of it as represented in Windsor. Perhaps the happiest of them all was Yvonne, who was dreaming of entertaining Charmian Daniels in her own little room. She thought she had a friend there, and from now on, things might look up. She would make her a cup of tea (not alcohol, drink meant little to Yvonne, but tea she did feel strongly about), and they would talk. In her way, Yvonne was a romantic.

Laraine saw it in terms of money. She usually did. In no abstract way, she was not a miser, but for what it could buy. Clothes, a bit of jewellery, a lover. She knew what she wanted, what was for sale and its price. She was for sale herself. Always had been, and her real grudge against life was that she hadn't fetched a higher price.

Nix heard trumpets blowing and saw flags flying. As she saw herself, she was a fighter against society. It was her against them. A battle by a woman for women. Show them.

Betty, as was her wont, weighed up the risks and profits of breaking the law, and came down in favour of breaking it. As she nearly always had done. It was the way of life of her family. Since she was out of touch with her brothers at the moment, she had substituted the other women, led by Laraine and Nix. She

70

would not necessarily remain loyal to them. Her loyalty was fragile, but for the moment they had it. She took Elsie Hogan with her as a kind of satellite: Elsie was not allowed, and did not want, her own opinions.

Rebecca knew she had got into it all because she had nowhere else to go. Anyway, she was a friend of Elsie Hogan who was a friend of Betty and she trusted them. As far as she trusted anyone. Why worry? She was a drifter, always had been, knew it and did not care. She was the despair of her probation officer.

Yvonne had not made a conscious choice. Once again, things were happening to her in a totally unexpected and mysterious way, and she just went along with them. She was the last one to know why.

Charmian Daniels found herself longing passionately for her little house in Deerham Hills, to which, she supposed, she would now never go back to live permanently. She would return only to sell and pack up. But it was no good, she would never get used to being a Southerner. North and South it was, just as in the days of Mrs Gaskell (one of her favourite novelists), and she was a Northerner. She felt unsophisticated and provincial and was annoyed with herself for feeling so. It was the girl Dolly who had made her feel like that, without meaning to but she had, with her glossy ways and her pretty voice. Also the young doctor with his superior manner.

Windsor society itself was probably too much for her and she had not bargained for the intensity of the Windsor season. She should never have come to live here, she should have left it to Anny who seemed better adjusted to it all (but Anny had always had money), and found herself some other hole to live in. Slough, say, or Staines.

Then she remembered Kate again and felt ashamed of herself. It was a terrible thing to be worried about your child. To suspect her of something you hardly dare think about. She had to respect this in Anny.

71

She looked at the address she had been given for Amanda Rivers, Kate's only girl friend in the district, saw that it was close to Wellington Yard, not out of her way, and decided to go there. Fast. Now.

She found herself in a street of small, flat-faced Victorian cottages, two up and two down, such as the artisans of the time had lived in. Now they were desirable properties. Amanda had a house with white shutters and a yellow front door with a dolphin for a knocker. The brass which should have been bright was dull and unpolished. No housekeeper then, or a long time away.

Charmian banged the knocker and sounded the bell. No answer. She could hear the noise sounding inside the house, but no one came. She stood back, looking up at the façade. The house was empty, no doubt about it, Amanda was not at home.

The door of the next house opened, and a head was poked round it. With surprise, Charmian recognised the face of one of the young actresses she had seen perform at the Theatre Royal. 'Oh do stop banging,' said the girl. 'I've been trying to get some rest. She's not there.'

'Do you know when she will be back?'

'Never, I should think.' The door was closing.

'I'm not the first to ask?' Charmian got in hastily.

'No, seems they are dead keen to see her at the hospital. Bye.' Now the door did close.

I'll be back, thought Charmian. It was interesting and agreeable to do her own leg work again, some time since she had. Academic research was, she now realised, a form of leg work. As she turned back towards Wellington Yard, Jerome and Elspeth were standing in the door of Jerome's shop. Oh, good, so she's back, she thought, glad for Jerome's sake. She had sensed strain in Jerome. They were deep in a conversation, but it was probably about work, because as she came up with them she heard Jerome say: 'Now take it easy. You've overdone it, but I forgive you, although some wouldn't. I'll say no more.'

'The baby is back,' she called out. 'Left outside the railway station. No one saw. His mother's got him now.'

'Thank goodness.' Jerome turned from Elspeth. 'Is he all right?'

'Got chicken-pox like his brother. But a light case.'

Having delivered her good news, Charmian went on to tell Anny and Jack.

She found Jack stone cold sober feeding black coffee to Anny who was not.

'They've got the baby back. The Robertson child.'

'Oh tell someone else,' said Anny. 'Go away.'

'I thought you'd be pleased.'

'Good news for others, when we have our own bad bundle, is not welcome,' said Jack softly. 'But thanks. When we both feel better we will be glad.'

'What is it then?' Charmian was anxious now. 'Tell me.'

'The police, your friends and colleagues, have found Kate's suitcase,' said Anny, in a dull, drunken voice that her friend had never heard before. 'With blood on it. All over blood. I saw it, identified it, so I know.'

Blood. Blood was all the same when it fell as a stain. Royal blood, plebeian blood, animal blood or Kate's blood, you could not tell the difference just by looking.

Chapter Seven

When from far away, never having been there, you thought about Windsor as a town and as an image, a piece of English history made solid, you might imagine the Castle, or the view of Eton Chapel across the river, or you might summon up a picture of the old Queen Victoria, the Widow of Windsor, as Kipling called her, driving through the town with her turbaned Indian servants by her side, but you did not think about the aeroplanes. When you were there though, you were only too conscious of them. Look up and you will see the great monsters rising through the sky from Heathrow, look down and the noise still fills your ears.

'Where was the bag found?' Charmian asked. An aeroplane roared across the sky and she went across the room to close the window.

'On a side road between Slough and Heathrow airport, just beyond Datchet,' said Jack. He was more in control of himself and the situation than Anny.

'Just on the roadside?' If that was the way, then it could not have been there long.

'No, a ditch runs along the road and it was in there.'

'Do you know who found it?' She knew she had a touch too much of her professional voice on her, but it was hard to change her manner in such matters after the careful years of learning it. Her friend picked it up at once.

'Oh shut up, Char,' said Anny wearily. 'You're asking too many questions.'

'It was a boy out with his dog,' said Jack.

It was always a boy with a dog.

'Anything else found? Any other possessions of Kate's?' Like a head or torso?

74

'I imagine they are looking. But you know all we were told.'
Charmian considered. 'Did you look inside the case, Anny?'
'Of course. Just clothes.'
'Could you identify any of them?'
'It was Kate's case, if that is what you mean. Her initials on it.
Besides, I gave it to her, and I know it. It was an expensive
affair from Vuittons. There wouldn't be many of those around
in a ditch in Berkshire.'
'No. What about the clothes?'
'I don't know quite what Kate has got, she's always buying
new stuff and dumping the old.'
'That's true,' said Jack. 'God's gift to Oxfam.'
'But I recognised her bathing costume. I gave her that too,
bought it in Milan when I was there last year.'
And you would not find two of those around in a hurry,
Charmian acknowledged.
She looked about the room, as of habit. She always liked to
study the background when questioning a suspect. Good God,
Anny wasn't that, she pushed the thought aside. No one could
suspect Anny.
Nevertheless, her eyes automatically retained the image of
the room in its disorder, as if no one had paid it much attention
lately, with books and papers on the chairs and dirty glasses on
the floor.
'We will have to see what is made of the case.' She sought for
comfort. 'Anyway, it doesn't look as though it can be Kate
holed up in that room in Ealing.'
Jack sat down heavily as if he was suddenly too big and
clumsy to stand. He looked beaten. 'That's coming to an end. It
was on the TV news. Shots fired. And a body thrown out on to
the street.'
'Oh you are cheering me up.' Anny reached out for the
whisky.
'It was the man, too,' said Jack, as if he could not stop
himself, but somehow guessed he was saying something
important: men could die at a woman's hand. Anny flinched.

They would be heading for one of their mammoth rows if someone did not stop them.

But Anny turned on her. 'Not much of a detective, are you? You haven't helped much with Kate, haven't found her. Got you to come here to help and you haven't.'

In spite of herself, Charmian was hurt. 'I didn't know I was got here for a purpose. But you needn't have worried, I'd have helped anyway. As I am doing.' She moved the whisky bottle away from Anny's hand.

If she had been heavy handed in mentioning the house in Ealing then Anny had handsomely paid her back.

'Take no notice,' said Jack. 'She's not herself. I'd have gone to identify the case myself if I'd been around but I wasn't.'

Off on one of those vague absences that seemed without purpose, but which filled his life.

'I was looking for her, Kate. Thought I might see her car,' he went on. 'I always think I might if I keep looking. See her car turning the corner. Or see her getting out of it. Or just walking down the road. Only I've got to keep on looking. Silly, isn't it?'

'No, Jack, not silly at all.' He loved his daughter more than Charmian had realised. Stupid of her. Not having a child made you maybe insensitive to parental love sometimes. For the first time she realised what she might have missed. But I'd have made a rotten mother, she told herself. 'Do you have any idea where Kate might be? Any guess to make?'

Jack shook his head. 'If I had, I'd have been there. Think I'd have waited around?'

'Did she never get in touch with you?' She gave a quick look towards Anny. There might be things Jack would not say in front of Anny.

'She did not,' he said heavily.

Anny stood up. 'You'd better leave us, Charmian. Let Jack and me sweat it out alone.'

'I'll see what I can do about the case and what it means. I'll find out more for you. Promise.' She had her own work to do, vital work with a time check on it, but this was important

76

too. Emotionally important to her.

Anny did not answer, she might not even have heard.

Jack came to the door with Charmian. Drawing it behind him, he said: 'What do you make of this case business?'

'I don't know, Jack, I really don't.'

'Looks bad to me.'

Charmian waited, there was something else.

'She did phone me once. About three weeks ago. Just after the two of them took off. Anny was out; I took the call. She was just starting to tell me something when Anny came back and grabbed the telephone. Kate rang off.' He looked at Charmian. 'Anny never told you?'

'No.' And Charmian could see why Anny had not mentioned it. 'Any clues where the call was from?'

'Well, I sort of wondered . . . ' Charmian waited. Not another railway station, as with the call to Anny? If it had been a railway station. 'It was a public place.' Here we go again, thought Charmian. 'It could have been a hospital,' he finished in a slow voice, as if he was still remembering what he had heard.

Charmian did not hesitate. 'Jack, go back in there and ask Anny if the call she took from Kate could also have been from a hospital.'

Without a word, Jack disappeared behind the door, leaving Charmian standing outside.

He was soon back. 'She says yes.'

Upstairs in her own place, Charmian fed Muff. 'It's a point about the hospital. If Jack's right, and I think he could be, then I really must get hold of Dr Amanda Rivers. She might know something. Kate could have been with her when she telephoned.' She stroked Muff's head bent over the bowl of liver. 'You are a disgusting eater, Muff. The hospital now, it's worth thinking about.' She yawned. 'You do the thinking, Muff, and I'll do the sleeping.'

It had been a hard day, and tomorrow was going to be worse. She had some searching interviews lined up with some travelling to do.

But tomorrow morning, before setting out, she would telephone Harold English and see what he could let her know about the case. He might not know much now but he could certainly find out.

'I bet the local lot are going over that ditch with a fine comb, Muff,' she said sleepily.

In the night, which was wet and warm, no searching was done, although the whole area was cordoned off. But with morning the search began again. It continued for some time, being conducted as thoroughly as Charmian had guessed.

The ditch turned at a right angle to the road and ran down a narrow track which led to a farm. The farm was owned by a syndicate which had built up a group of farms in the neighbourhood. No one lived in the farmhouse.

Nothing more was found at that time.

Charmian was told this when she telephoned Harold English from a booth in the main post office which was better for her purpose than using either Anny's or Jerome's. (He had made the offer.) Neutral territory, she thought, and no listening ears. Jerome was not neutral. Better to be alone.

Not quite true, as she gazed around at the crowd of locals posting parcels or getting their pensions cashed, while jostling with the tourists stamping picture postcards of the Queen or her Castle, but none of them were bothering with what she was saying.

'What about this case?'

'Found by a lad out walking. I expect you know that.' He was mildly sardonic. 'The initials on it were interesting, so Mrs Cooper was asked to take a look. She identified it as her daughter's.'

'And is there blood on it?'

'A few stains only. Nothing much, so I am told.'

Anny had exaggerated then, but she could be forgiven for that.

'So what's going on?' The sound of an aeroplane overhead almost drowned her out, but he knew what she was saying, had been prepared for her question.

'That's Concorde going over. Can't mistake it, can you? In answer to you, the bloodstains are being tested for grouping.'

'Is a connection being made between the case and the severed limbs?'

'Let's say the idea is being kicked around.'

Charmian drew further into the booth to get the maximum shelter. Next to her a large lady was having a struggle to get the number she wanted. 'Can you hear? I don't want to shout. I think it would be worth finding out if a doctor in one of the local hospitals knows anything about the case and where Kate Cooper is or has been. I think they may have been together. I'll give you the details.'

Then they got down to the hard business, the material Harold English was really interested in. After a preliminary discussion in which Charmian told him what she had done on the day before, and what she planned to do today. He was her helper, her channel of communication, but he was also a check on her, a kind of invigilator. She recognised this as a fact, half resenting it.

'Yes, get on with seeing them at home. Very valuable. Want any help?'

'Not with that. I have them lined up. But I'm interested in the link with Delaney. I think he is passing them money. Someone is. I think Laraine is the paymaster.' It was her opinion that sums of money passed through Laraine's hands with degrees of generosity, more staying with Laraine and Nix than filtered through to, say, Yvonne. Her new shoes had not cost anything near the price of Laraine's new suit. 'Can you run a check on them?'

'Probably,' he agreed cautiously. 'They don't sound the sort to run bank accounts.'

'Try post office accounts, possibly in either Windsor or Slough. Or they could be using a building society. One of the bigger ones, I guess. Not under their own names.' She did not

79

believe Laraine let them float around in liquid cash. She would make them hide it away.

They made arrangements to meet.

The woman in the next booth had abandoned her attempts to dial the number she wanted and had turned to shouting at the operator.

'Chicago. I am calling Chicago.' She did not seem to be getting anywhere.

Charmian emerged from her booth to offer her help. The woman turned to her gladly.

'I am trying to dial Chicago.'

'Can you dial Chicago from Windsor?'

'Yes, yes, yes,' cried the woman.

'Let me try.' Charmian squeezed into the narrow area and took up the telephone. It went dead.

Dolly and Len were also talking on the telephone.

'Was it as good for you last night as it was for me?' asked Dolly.

'Dolly, you shock me.'

'And don't I enjoy doing it.' Dolly was exuberant. Their relationship was going to take off, she knew it. Might even turn out to be important.

'Apart from anything else, how much time did we have before the bleeper went off?'

Dolly giggled. 'Time enough. You'll see.'

'Now you've shocked me again.'

She loved it when that exasperated, ever so slightly pompous note came into his voice. She loved his voice. He didn't know that, of course. Probably thought he was adored for quite other things.

'I'm very interested in what you had to say about the way the taken babies are fed.'

'Might be,' said the future top consultant cautiously. 'Only a suggestion.' He was almost regretting saying anything to Dolly.

'No, it's brilliant of you. I had no idea such things could be.

I'm going to work on it.' Quietly, putting herself ahead, and not letting a colleague get a nose in until she decided when. 'Means looking for a special type of person.' She thought she could do it, too. Also there had to be people who knew, one person, perhaps more than one, who had given advice.

Len confirmed this idea. 'There would have to be a professional involved somewhere.'

'One of your lot?'

'Could be.' A slight unease crept into his voice.

'Who's the most likely?'

His mind ran over his colleagues. In alphabetical order – he had an orderly mind – he assembled a list: Brent, Cadwallader, Merrilee, Prosser, Rivers. Those were the most likely names to have been called upon to give such advice. They all worked in the relevant field. Although a GP might have done so. He could make cautious enquiries, and then he would consider what to tell Dolly. If he read that young woman aright, she could be ruthless in pursuit of her aims.

'I'll let you know,' he said to Dolly, 'when I've had time to consider.'

'I'm on duty tonight.'

'And I'm on call again,' Len said sadly; they were terribly undermanned at the moment, people ill, people taking exams and people away who jolly well should be back.

Dolly finished the telephone call by announcing that she would be cooking a large steak on the evening after, and if he liked to join her in eating it, then he would be welcome. She had a strong idea he was not a vegetarian.

'You can bring some red wine and do the washing up,' and she put the telephone down. Start as you mean to go on.

Sooner or later, he would give her that list of names. She intended he should.

Then she would take action. The follower of Charmian Daniels could do no less.

Charmian Daniels, unaware that she was both an example and

81

an inspiration, moved forward into her working day. She had fed the cat, drunk some coffee, and bought a newspaper from Brian Robertson who had a broad smile and said mother and two kids might be home this week. Peter was better and had told the police, Yes, he did see a lady standing over the plastic sack, but he did not see her face. She was wearing blue trousers and a yellow top, and he thought she had fair hair.

They didn't get much out of that then, she decided as she walked away, wondering, as they all were, whether the boy was telling the truth or how much of it. Might have a word with him myself some time. His father believes him, but it will be the mother who will know. Might not say, of course, but would certainly know.

Charmian went back into the shop to buy a box of chocolates. She was going to see Yvonne first and Yvonne seemed a person who would appreciate a present, and did not get many. If ever she had seen a woman who had failed to get the fairy off the Christmas tree, it was Yvonne.

Yvonne also had made her preparations. She greeted her visitor with a bright smile, and led her inside. Her hair, pretty hair once, but grey now, was washed and well sprayed with lacquer. Another new pair of shoes was on her feet, and she had the teatray ready.

Her home was in one room. The teatray was on the table that also served as desk and dressing table. On almost every surface Yvonne's clothes and small possessions were distributed. She was impartial, apparently not minding if her nightgown occupied a chair with a packet of biscuits. Several pairs of shoes, all new, shared a hiding place with a bottle of milk.

'Been here long?' asked Charmian, handing over the chocolates.

'About two weeks,' admitted Yvonne shyly. 'It's taking me a bit of time to get settled in.' She glanced around her in a puzzled way. 'I don't seem to get on top of it somehow.' She removed a pair of shoes from beside the milk bottle and replaced it with a packet of teabags. This piece of housekeeping satisfied her, she resumed her smile and turned to Charmian. 'Thank you ever so much for the chocolates. You'll take a cup of tea?'

The sad thing about Yvonne was that as you talked to her you became aware that she was a person who had once had, even if she had now forgotten it, some education. You could tell it from the shape and pattern of her speech, and the way she poured the tea.

Charmian had the tape recorder going. Yvonne said she did not mind, she seemed flattered at the idea she was on record. After some innocuous routine questions, Charmian said: 'Do you like prison?'

'No.' Yvonne was surprised. 'No one could.'

'But you keep going back.'

Yvonne turned on her much the look she had offered to her muddled room. 'It's not that I feel at home there,' she tried to explain. 'That would be a terrible thing to say.' She struggled to get it right. 'I know how to behave there. People tell you what to do. I don't seem to know outside.'

Incompetent, lost, with no one to tell her what to do, and no money, Yvonne eventually performed the acts that sent her back to that safe haven.

Charmian knew her record and knew that she had long periods of going straight before going back inside. She always committed what might be called a public crime, shoplifting or robbing a till. She never took from a private purse. She had her standards.

'When did you last see your children?'

Yvonne looked vague. 'I'd like to write . . . ' Probably dyslexic, thought Charmian. That may always have been her trouble. Or part of it. 'But I've got my friends.'

Yes, Charmian could see why Yvonne wanted Laraine and Nix and Co. But why did they want her?

Or had she just hung on? Charmian was beginning to recognise an adhesive quality to Yvonne that might make her difficult to dislodge. Not that Laraine struck her as a compassionate heart.

83

'They helped me get this room.' She looked around with that mixture of satisfaction in her own achievement in having done anything at all and bewilderment at not having done it better that Charmian was beginning to recognise as characteristic of her. 'I come from round here. Went to school. Grew up. My old teacher Miss Macy still knows me.' There was pride in her voice. A long relationship was obviously unusual.

'That's nice.' It was an encouraging noise so that she would go on talking.

'We're helping,' said Yvonne shyly. 'You should help other people, shouldn't you?'

'If you can. What do you do?'

'She has a charity that gives outings to disabled children. It's nice for them. She's taking them to the Fair in the Great Park. We'll help her with that.'

'Will you now?' The thought of Laraine and Nix, not to mention Baby, on such expeditions was something to grapple with.

Yvonne seemed to read her mind. 'Laraine was keen straight away and told the others they must be,' she said proudly. 'When Miss Macy visited me inside and told me what she did and I told Laraine she said straight away, That's it and told the others so.'

Charmian sipped her tea; it was good. Yvonne had done her job well.

Betty Dedman and Elsie Hogan shared a small flat while Rebecca Amos lived in a guest house round the corner from them. It was not a place of luxury, more of a working man's hostel than a four star hotel, thus confirming Charmian's view that a certain selectivity operated in the doling out of funds.

Betty and Elsie had a small but nice establishment, with a hopeful air of permanence to it. They were planting window boxes. Of course, they both had jobs, while Rebecca, perhaps from choice, did not.

Not being tea drinkers they offered her whisky or sweet

84

sherry. She chose the whisky. It was a good brand. In one corner of the room was a box stacked with bottles of squash, cans of Coke and packets of potato crisps.

Betty saw Charmian looking at them. 'For some kids we know,' she said briefly.

'The Great Park outing?'

'Yes.' Betty gave her a sharp look. 'Who told you?' Then she answered herself. 'Yvonne.'

'It's very good of you.' And it was giving Charmian cause to think. She was trying to put together a picture. A jigsaw or a mosaic: there were several pieces still missing.

'I'm not a child lover,' said Betty, stating what was obvious, 'but you've got to do what you can. I get the goods from the supermarket where I work.'

'Does Elsie work there too?' She adjusted a tape. 'I'm recording this, you don't mind?'

'What you like.' Betty did not care. Elsie Hogan did not answer, no need, Betty was her voice. 'Else works in the butcher's division.'

'Nice job,' said Charmian absently.

'You think so, do you? Hear that, Else, you've got a nice job.' Elsie did not answer. 'And in case you are asking, the reason I keep going back to prison is because I keep getting caught. The times I don't get caught, I don't go inside. I'm a professional. Got that?'

Charmian nodded. Laraine was a bit of a feminist, Nix was an individualist, Elsie was silent, and Yvonne was lonely. Betty was doing a job.

That was her claim, anyway.

'You're being very honest. Do you mind if I quote you?'

'Suit yourself,' said Betty indifferently.

Charmian sipped her whisky. It seemed to burn her tongue.

Rebecca Amos, the only one not to be in work, was the only one not to have stayed at home to meet her as arranged. There was no Rebecca and no sign of anyone at the house to tell Charmian where she was. It was the sort of hotel where you

85

could be missing for days before anyone noticed you were gone.

Charmian was totally unsurprised at being let down. She had met this sort of treatment before. Every so often with this lot, they led you up to a door, then shut it in your face. Not exactly unreliable, although it often felt like that, more unpredictable. The uncertainty syndrome, she called it, and perhaps it was the most significant thing she had noticed about them. It was something they all shared, even Baby.

She did not hold it against them, she had felt like being less disciplined herself. Perhaps they were more honest and spontaneous than she was. Or just braver.

Passing a small public garden, not far from the hotel, she saw Rebecca Amos sitting on a bench in the sun, enjoying the warmth like a small cat with no real home.

Charmian walked across, and sat down beside her. After a bit, she looked up. 'Oh it's you. Might have known you'd find me. Well, I don't want to talk.'

'That's all right.'

'No, it's not. You've taken the others in, but you don't take me in. You're up to something. I may not be clever, but I can tell that much.'

'I don't think I've taken anyone in,' said Charmian mildly. She had not overlooked this herself. 'I ask questions, you answer them. Or not. I'm interested.'

Rebecca started to laugh. 'First time I've ever been paid money for doing nothing.'

'Nothing?'

'Feels like nothing. Just taking a pack of kids on outings.'

While this was happening a police team was searching the ditch where the suitcase had been found. They had provisionally identified it now as belonging to Kate Cooper. They extended their search to the ditch as it ran up the side road to the farmhouse.

It was a difficult, dirty job since the ditch seemed to have been used as a deposit for old rubbish for some decades. There were several old cycles, more than one pram, tin cans, bottles and plastic bags without number, and even parts of an old car.

By this time, with a skill in excavating and assessing the age of rubbish that an archaeologist would have envied, the police had established that the severed limbs had been deposited in the refuse tip on a day previous to the discovery of the limbs in Wellington Yard. They were about to undertake the same process of dating for the woman's case.

The searchers, hot and tired, decided that the boy and the dog had had it easy.

Then, beneath an old mattress which itself had been covered with branches from a torn-up bush, they discovered another suitcase.

This one had belonged to a man.

Chapter Eight

'What you've got to remember,' said Lady Oriel, 'is that we are all fascinated by the murder. Two murders, in fact, it has to be so because of the legs belonging to a man and a woman. It's no good pretending that Anny won't be stared at, because she will, but she must come to the Fair and stick it out.' This was Molly Oriel's philosophy of life. When bad things happened you faced them and stared them out.

This was not how everyone felt, not exactly how Charmian felt herself, experience had taught her that from some happenings you did well to walk away, run, if you could.

'She happens to agree with you,' she said. 'But it's tough. So that's why I am with her.'

'It's her own fault really, for shouting so loudly about Kate.'

'Only to her friends.'

'My dear,' said Molly Oriel, laying her hand on Charmian's wrist. 'In matters of this sort, there are no friends.' She gave Charmian a frank look. Not even me, she might have been saying.

They were sitting side by side in the sun on a seat in the Great Park. All around them the Fair was assembling itself. Across the way from where the two women were sitting, a hot-dog stand was frying onions. Next door a soft drinks stall was already selling cans of Coke to a queue of little boys in Wolf Cubs uniform, whose own stall, a tombola, in aid of their own organisation, had been set out to await their first customer. Bottles and tins of all sorts were arranged in piles, and every number in the dip won you something. A tin of apricot jam from Hungary, a bottle of home-made rhubarb wine, a tin of orange juice, or if you were lucky a bottle of sherry. Both Charmian and Molly had promised to buy tickets the moment

88

this stall was declared officially opened. They were awaiting the arrival of Lavender Bell, their pack leader.

Next to this stall was a big hut selling hats, shoes and boots for the country dweller. Rubber boots and shoes from Korea hung on one display wall, jostling trilby hats in all colours for both sexes, and panama hats with bright silk lining. There was also a counter of sweatshirts decorated by pigs' faces with flashing eyes. Red blinking eyes. There were others that squeaked.

Two lines of stalls, booths and caravans stretched between the trees. You could buy china on one stall, jewellery on another and candy floss on another. A row of coloured lights hung in loops between the trees, ready to be switched on when night fell. Then the bonfire would be lit. The day was going to end with a giant barbecue and a concert.

A junior member of the royal family was coming to open the Fair. In the distance the royal car could be seen arriving.

Molly Oriel stood up. 'Come on, let's go and curtsey. I love that bit. Nice hat she's got on. We go to the same milliner, you know.'

Hard to tell with Molly, Charmian thought, when she was joking or not. Probably not this time. 'Lucky you.'

'His prices have trebled, my dear, since he has got so smart.'

The car came level with them, they made their bobs, and rose. Molly's performance was elegantly done; with Charmian it was a little more clumsy.

Anny came striding through the crowds. 'There you are, thought you were meant to be helping me.'

'We have been. I personally tacked your background hessian into place, and I have the bruises to prove it.' Molly Oriel held out a hand whose delicately pink-tipped fingers looked immaculate. A great diamond glittered on her left hand. Molly did not believe in dressing down.

Anny, however, looked distinctly the worse for wear. Dark spectacles hid her eyes and her clothes were crumpled as though they had been slept in, which was probably the case, because

Charmian recognised them from yesterday. A mark of Anny's disorientation. Charmian knew it and Molly Oriel guessed. 'Go and comb your hair, Anny. I happen to know HRH is coming to your stall. I fixed it myself. Who's looking after it now?'

'I left Jack. But I'm afraid he's had a drop this morning.'

'Of course.' Molly was totally unsurprised.

Anny obeyed her silent advice. 'Yes, I'd better get back.' A drunk Jack was unpredictable.

Charmian said: 'I'll come too.' On her own she found Molly Oriel daunting company; she had such an air of bringing with her worldly contacts and understandings that were outside Charmian's sphere. In short, every so often, she felt put in her place. In spite of this she liked the woman. They left Molly making her deft way towards the illustrious party, flinging over her shoulder, 'I see it's Susan today. Such a dear, I must say hello to her.'

After the tombola (now doing a brisk trade), they passed a stall set inside a tent where two young women, one blonde, one very dark, both tall and slender, were busy pinning up a notice: ARIADNE KNITS. All around them were spread sweaters, dresses and shawls in glorious jewel colours. The women themselves were dressed in their own wares to which their figures did full justice.

'Lose a pound or two and I could wear those,' murmured Anny. 'Good colours. That's Ariadne Vernon and her sister Meta. They were into their earth colours last season, which frankly I found too quiet. I prefer this new range. I met them at the Windsor Horse Show last month. We had stalls side by side then. Wish I had now, they are such a draw, always bring the crowds along.'

Ariadne saw them and waved. 'Come on over for coffee later if you've got time.'

Anny smiled and waved back. 'Shan't go. She's bound to ask after Kate. They were chums.'

In the middle distance they could see Molly Oriel's bright dress dipping again in an obeisance, and then her figure turning

90

and twisting in animated conversation. She was a tall woman and she stood out.

Anny said: 'Stop here for a minute, I want to say something: Jack is sure that the clothes in the case do not belong to our Katy.'

'You thought so yourself.' Although you did not say so.

'Yes, I suppose so,' admitted Anny reluctantly. 'What I do know,' and Anny's voice was serious, 'is that the swimsuit was certainly Kate's. I have a feeling I never saw the other clothes before, but what does that mean?'

Charmian considered. It might not mean much. But it had to be taken into the account. Perhaps Kate had more than one life. One into which she had now disappeared, taking Harry with her. That was quite a thought. The clothes belonged in that life. It did not sound like the Kate she had known as a child, but people grew up. She did not know this Kate now.

'Try and make up your mind about the clothes, Anny. It might be important. Have you told anyone but me?'

'No,' Anny's seriousness deepened. 'I want you to try and find out. Someone has to, I can see that, and I think it ought to be you. Because if those are not Kate's clothes, then whose are they? And why is Kate's bathing suit there?'

And once again, where is Kate? As Charmian did not say aloud.

'There is someone walking around without any clothes,' said Anny. 'Or not walking around. Cut up in pieces and left around for us to find. That's the most likely, isn't it?'

'As yet, no one knows for sure if the case is connected with either of the limbs.' Or the limbs with Kate.

'Oh, that's just talking like a policeman. Now talk with your heart.'

'Well, all right. Yes, in my heart, as you put it, I do believe that the case will turn out to be connected with the limbs. And yes, I do believe that Kate comes into it somewhere.'

Anny drew in a deep breath. 'Thanks for being honest.' And as she did not say: At last.

91

'I've always been honest with you, Anny.'

'Oh, in the way of friendship, perhaps, but now I see what deviousness you are capable of I am not so sure.'

Charmian flushed. There was Anny doing it again. Sometimes she picked things up as from the air. Charmian could remember the time that Anny had told her that if she thought she was going to be a teacher of history in a top girls' school (which was where Charmian truly believed she was heading), then she was walking in the opposite direction. Two months later, Charmian had joined the Force. Even later there was the time she pointed out to an incredulous Charmian that her marriage did not really suit what she was. That turned out to be a fact, too.

What did she see now?

'Being a successful policewoman has corrupted you, Charmian.'

'Damn you, Anny.' She showed her hurt. 'I do my job. And do it to the best of my ability. And if I've been successful, well, good. I don't accept that it has harmed me.'

'Well, hasn't it? I know you, my girl. You've got that pinched look about you. Isn't there something in your life at this moment that you would rather there wasn't?'

Charmian was silent.

'Is it to do with Humphrey?'

'No,' she said quickly. And yet it was, and she knew it, and as she spoke, Anny knew it too.

Anny shrugged. 'I see I am right. Is he in love with you? Or you with him? Is that it?'

'No.'

'You must need someone.'

'Speak for yourself.' In matters of sex they had never seen eye to eye.

'I'm not convinced.'

'Nothing like that. Don't ask any more, please, Anny.'

They had arrived at Anny's stall just a pace or two ahead of the Princess and her party, who were still at the next stall, but in time to see Jack waver forward to the Princess with hands outstretched.

'Ma'am,' he made a deep swaying bow, lost his balance and went over.

He got to his feet quickly. When drunk Jack was nimble and very determined. He still had it in mind to attack the royal presence.

Charmian got her arm round him and jerked him back, just in time. 'Don't be such a fool.'

'Let me go.' Jack tried to drag away.

Anny had moved to the front of her stall protectively, as if this was what really mattered.

A plainclothes policeman appeared from the bushes behind the stall and put a heavy restraining hand on Jack who was still sending out an incoherent stream of protests.

'Not going to hurt her. Just ask her. Kate's still missing. People are forgetting. Need help.'

Between them, Charmian and the security man got him round the back of Anny's stall to where her car stood.

'Thanks.' Charmian got her breath back. 'Don't make anything of this. He didn't mean any harm. He's just drunk.'

The royal party, protected and impervious, had finished its purchases at the stall next door to Anny's (the Women's Institute, jam and shortbread), and led by Molly Oriel were moving on. Anny stepped into position with a smile. Jack was still mouthing, but silently, from the rear of the car, and making no attempt to escape. They ignored him.

Charmian said: 'A good thing you turned up. Didn't see you.'

'Oh, you're not meant to. We're all about. I've got several colleagues pretending to be a tree.'

Charmian gave Jack a look. He had gone quiet. 'He's harmless.'

'I know that.' He was brisk, dismissive. 'I'm not worrying about him.'

'Who does worry you then?'

He laughed. 'Well, let's say I am not worried about old ladies with thermos flasks and their knitting.' He moved into the background. 'Keep your friend under control, though.'

Charmian returned for a look at Jack who was slumped in sullen silence, eyes half closed. He opened them to deliver a sour glance, then turned away.

Charmian got into the car, and sat there with him.

'What's up, Jack? Something is.'

'You know.'

'Something more.'

He did not answer but gave one of his rolling groans as if he was sorry for himself and meant to go on being sorry for himself.

'You're a fool, Jack.' Charmian was irritated, as she always was with Jack in this state, no sympathy from her. 'A bloody fool to do what you did just now.'

This got under his skin as she had meant it to. 'I know something you don't know.'

'Probably you do. So what?' She wanted to bang his drunken head. She had never been able to stand drunks.

'I get about. Meet people. Have drinks. Talk. People talk back.'

'I know that, Jack.' Every friend of Jack and Anny knew it, knew his habits, how he sought out his favourite pubs, visiting one after the other in a determined but haphazard way, like a dog looking for the right street corners. You could never count on him being in any particular pub, but in one of them he would be, picking up casual drinking friends to whom he then gave a devoted if transient attention. He had his hours, largely shaped by the licensing laws. Out of those hours, if he did not fancy to drink alone, or Anny had her eye on him, then he had what he called 'his club'. No club. He kept a bottle with a friend who had a shoe-shop, and together they would often share a reviving nip. They had nothing in common except a feeling that a drink shared made a bond. But that was the way with all Jack's drinking friends. You could never see why he liked them or even if he did.

94

Anny, who knew and resented every one of them, called them Jack's doggy friends.

Now a doggy friend had obviously spoken. Come up with something that Jack longed to talk about but feared to do so. Charmian was a safe receptacle.

'This chap, a policeman, not a high-up like you, ordinary chap, but he gets to know things.'

Someone with a minor desk job, Charmian speculated, but at the centre where information was passed around. Such a man would hear the gossip.

'Go on, Jack.'

'Found another suitcase. A man's this time. Aha, you didn't know that.'

'No, but I'm not surprised.' Two dead people, two cases.

'And the man's case has been opened, sorted over with a bloody hand. Blood on the clothes inside. Been grouped. Same group as the man's limbs, so it's probably his blood. Chap didn't know the type for sure, but thought it was A. Not Kate's.'

'Well, that's good.' Or was it?

'But it is Harry's. Saw his blood donor card. Remembered.'

'Still a common group,' said Charmian thoughtfully.

'It's his all right.' Jack spoke with conviction, as if he had had a message that could not be denied. 'His case, his blood. So the other one has to be Kate's. I was wrong about the clothes.'

'I'm not sure if you were.' His first spontaneous reaction might well be the truest one. Unconsciously, he had known, not the clothes, maybe, but his daughter's taste. What he had really been saying was: Those are not the sort of clothes Kate would choose.

'All right. Say I wasn't wrong. Where does that leave us?'

It was a valid question.

Three people dead perhaps? Another woman as well as Kate? I won't think that, she said to herself.

'Leave it to me. I'll be able to find out more, Jack.'

He turned away with a shrug. She knew more or less what the shrug meant: We have left it too long already.

95

At Anny's stall the royal party, having paused politely to allow some photographs and to talk to some children, had arrived and were being welcomed by Anny, pale and tense, but in control of herself.

She motioned to Charmian: 'Come and help me.' She was more nervous than she looked.

As Charmian came forward, Anny said under her breath: 'Thanks for that. I could kill Jack.' Then she caught Molly Oriel's eye and moved smoothly forward.

Five minutes later Anny looked flushed and pretty, her troubles momentarily behind her.

'Made a sale: the yellow lion with the orange beard, and half a promise to look in at the London show.' For the minute, just for the minute, she had forgotten Kate.

Then the memory came rushing back. 'What was that with you and Jack? When you were sitting in the car.'

So she had watched.

'Just talk. Let him tell you.'

Anny looked at her suspiciously. 'I hate it when people know something I don't.'

'We all do.'

'It's about Kate, of course. Not much else you two would talk about.'

It was true Jack and Charmian had never had much in common, but they had learnt how to behave to each other.

Then Anny's mood lightened. 'I'm glad the Robertsons have got their baby back. But did you know he had chicken-pox too? Poor little soul.'

A crowd surged around Anny's stall, she was suddenly in business. A royal visit has that effect.

Charmian left her to it and strolled off, ready to enjoy a woodland interlude. She needed a breathing space, just to be ordinary for once, not watching people, being suspicious.

The Fair was taking place in a bosky hollow in the Great Park, tall trees curving overhead, almost meeting, with wooded vistas behind. Along one avenue was a distant view of a house, white, glimmering in the sun, romantic.

The ancient hunting ground of English kings was turned now into gentle parkland, as poised and arranged as if Capability Brown himself had set it out. Nature was imitating art copying nature.

Hustle and bustle spread itself up and down the clearing. The merry-go-round had started to swing. Charmian could see a swan slowly revolving with a small child stuck to its neck. Behind the swan a wooden horse rose and fell with a gondola coming into sight behind. Two children sat knee to knee in the boat. With the two children was Laraine, knees hunched up under her chin, a set smile on her face. She was not enjoying the ride.

Behind the gondola swung a red London two decker with room for one inside, and two on top. With a boy and a girl was Nix.

Yvonne was in the next vehicle, a train dragging two wooden carriages with GWR painted on them. She was shepherding four youngsters. They looked happy and so did she.

Laraine came into view again then, anxiously rubbing the skirt of her best suit. Something had stained it. Perhaps from the ice-cream cornet her fellow passengers were eating.

From behind a tree, Charmian studied the scene.

Elsie and Rebecca were not far away. She was not surprised to see them there too, standing side by side in company with an elderly woman of friendly appearance, who was just drawing a large thermos flask from a basket. Miss Macy, no doubt of it, Yvonne's old teacher and friend. She was surrounded by a bunch of children. From a distance they looked normal happy children, but one or two were sitting down as if they felt happier near the ground and one boy was wearing heavy surgical boots.

Here they were then, with their group of disabled children, kindly helping to amuse them. Baby, she noticed, was not there. Baby had a real gift for virtuously not doing anything she did not wish.

But the others? Why were they here? It was a scene to

provoke thought. Yvonne she could understand. Even Nix. Elsie and Rebecca counted for nothing. They were just padding.

But Laraine? Laraine did nothing without a purpose.

She stared at Charmian, and Charmian could read the message, defiant, arrogant, bold: There you are, pig, and here am I. Make what you can of it.

'I could read it as well as if she'd said it aloud,' Charmian told Harold English later that day.

'Mustn't get too imaginative,' he said. He found Charmian Daniels' free flights into fancy alarming; she had done it once or twice in their short acquaintance and it was not his style at all. But he had been told to trust her and so he did. 'I think the time has come for a case conference,' he said. Strictly speaking, it was for Charmian to ask for one, but he doubted she would.

Nor did she. 'No, I'm not ready.'

'You are not required to present a thesis to us. But I'd say you'd got enough to talk about.'

Doubtfully, she said: 'I know who; I think I am beginning to think I know what. But I do not know when or why. I have to know why.'

Harold English said to himself that was her all over. He thought the important thing was when.

The problem of the recidivist women and the case of the carved up bodies, which might or might not have a connection with Kate and Harry, started to move at almost the same moment, as if some hidden string bound the two together so that a tug at one pulled at the other. Whether this was chance or not, only time would show.

Charmian took the advice of Harold English and called a conference. In matters of this sort, she felt he knew what was what. It was her first experience of work in such a sensitive area. One did not, he was implying, hang about.

The conference was held, as before, in London with the same

people present. Afterwards, Charmian, although she had taken careful notes, found that because of the unpleasant events of later in the day, she had very patchy memories of what went on.

Humphrey presided, if that was quite the word for such an informal meeting over sandwiches and drinks. All the same, he definitely had his hand on the wheel and meant to guide their little ship into some port or other.

Charmian spoke and they listened to her.

'And so you're convinced that there is a definite plan?'

'Yes.' She nodded. 'My informant,' Beryl Andrea Barker, 'had always implied it.' Nothing definite. Hints were more in Baby's line, but she knew how to get her message across. 'She was sure enough to get in touch with me.'

'Borne out by our local contact,' said Humphrey. 'He really put his finger on it. Interesting the way things have built up. You've been in touch?'

Charmian nodded. She did not amplify it, she was in frequent contact and Humphrey must know this fact.

Harold English cleared his throat. 'You're well placed there for a quiet talk.' So she was, Charmian thought.

'So what do you conclude? What's the project?' Humphrey looked at her.

'Wish I knew for sure. I don't think they know themselves. No, let me correct that. I don't think the upper echelon and the lower of that group know the same thing. I believe that Yvonne and Rebecca and Elsie believe they are planning a demo in support of all women prisoners, something like that. I would say that children came into it somehow and that they were looking over the Great Park as a venue.'

Humphrey seemed relieved. 'That doesn't sound too dangerous.'

'That's their notion. I think the other two, Nix and Laraine, have different plans. I think Nix is out for blood. One way or another. But Laraine . . . Somehow there is money in it for Laraine. She would do anything for enough cash. I don't think any deal would be too dirty for her.'

'You sound as though you admire her.'

'Not admire, no.' No, there was a coldness, a selfishness about Laraine that cut into you. 'But respect as a force, yes. She's formidable.'

Humphrey said: 'We can't risk leaving her on the loose now we know she had contact with a possible IRA connection.'

'Yes, she's the paymaster.' Charmian had in front of her a list of the investments which the group had in various building societies. They had not after all used false names. As she had guessed, some were considerably richer than others, with Laraine being the best off.

'The man Delaney is being watched, I take it? We know where he is and what he is doing?'

A voice from the back of the room, a small dark Welshman who represented another security department: 'He's behaving normally. Even driving the kids to school. Too bloody normal for my liking.'

'We'll have to take them all in.' Harold English spoke up. 'Find an excuse. Shouldn't be difficult.'

'What about the man?'

'Take him in too.'

A dead silence fell on the room.

Charmian heard her own voice. 'No. That will bugger things up. If we do that, then we will never find out what was planned. And it could happen later. We have to hang in there and find out. Now.'

'You got away with that,' said Harold English. He said it half admiringly, half doubtfully. 'Seems dangerous to me.'

'Oh, Humphrey will see the security side is wrapped up.' No one doubted that. 'And the other way would be the greater risk.'

'Yes, he's on your side.' It was said appraisingly, thoughtfully, as if the matter had been weighed up and found to be so. Charmian never doubted that it had been and by others than Harold English.

100

'Humphrey doesn't take sides. But he had to trust me on this and he did.' Besides, he had put her into the job, he owed her loyalty.

'Worked with him before, have you?'

She nodded. That case wouldn't bear talking about. Not by her, anyway, because Humphrey's own son had been involved and he was dead now.

'Give me a lift back, will you? My wife drove me in but she kept the car to go and see her mother.'

He had an endlessly convenient wife, Charmian thought, who was always out of the way when he wanted her to be.

'Of course.'

He tucked his bulk comfortably into her car. 'As long as you're sure what you're doing with these women, I'd like a look at them myself. I never seem to get that.'

'Oh sure, who's sure? But I think I can find out. And as for seeing them, I'm meeting them in the bar of the Rose and Garter this evening. Come and take a look, but don't let them see you. They know a policeman when they see one.' She added with helpful malice: 'Bring your wife if she's back.'

'What are you going to do with them?'

'Take them for a group photograph at Joe King's photographer's shop across the road.'

Harold English looked at her and decided she meant it.

'Has it struck you that they might be stringing you along?'

'I'm sure that they think they are.' Or those among them that did any thinking. 'But Beryl Barker, Andrea,' she added out of respect for Baby's feelings, 'was clear that something major was planned. And I have a lot of respect for Barker's instinct for self-preservation.' Her intuition had told her that there was something brewing within the group that would spell danger to Baby if she didn't put herself in the clear.

'There's a note in your voice as if you sympathise with them.'

'Not me.'

'Understand, then?'

'Not that either. Wouldn't dare. Empathise a bit, perhaps.'

101

Even with Laraine. One of those hard women who, in the end, hurt themselves more than anybody.

He decided again that she meant what she said.

As they sped across flyovers and down the M4, passing slower traffic and avoiding hold-ups, he said: 'That other business. You asked me to see what I could get on the man Harry.'

'And?'

'He hasn't been sighted. Nor the girl Kate. But a bit of background . . . He's been in and out of hospital more than once after violent incidents. People seem to bash him somehow. One of those people.' There were such, as all policemen knew. 'Got a fair amount of money, though. That's interesting. Inherited wealth.'

'So they could be anywhere? Is that what you are saying?'

'Have money, could travel.'

Her speed increased.

'You're in a hurry.'

She slowed down a little. 'Sorry, am I driving too fast? I have something I want to do before I see the Girls.'

'Oh?'

With a sideways look, she said: 'I'm going to see a doctor.'

He decided she meant that too.

Policewoman Dolly Barstow was looking for a doctor too. Len had come across with his list of names of those who might have given certain advice to the baby kidnapper. Dolly had known she would get it, but he had been tougher than she had expected and she had promised discretion. Her idea of discretion was an immediate call on the most likely doctor.

As she drove to the chosen address she passed a van-load of her colleagues coming back from the farm where the two cases had been found. Almost her heart bled for them, they were working like dogs down there, turning everything over, and finding nothing so she'd heard. No bodies, not a clue, just farm muck and mud. And it was raining.

Without knowing it, she passed Charmian Daniels heading

102

towards home after depositing Harold English at his house. Neither woman observed the other.

Charmian had one call to fit in before trying to find Dr Amanda Rivers at home. She had a message for her 'contact'. He was an easy man to meet.

'Just to tell you that I am getting the group photograph you wanted. You may have it tomorrow.' The Girls had raised no objection; it was wanted for her thesis. 'That as well,' she told herself.

There was never any need to say much. In an underground kind of way these two understood each other. They were not friends but they might have been very much more. There were destined to be shocks ahead.

'I may remember something else if I see them all together,' He was a man of many parts who might have encountered any one of the women in his career at various points. It was interesting he still felt himself a law enforcer.

He had a strong sense, he informed her, of natural justice. He hated to let people get away with things.

'I shouldn't think you did very often.'

'Not if I can help it.'

He gave Charmian an assessing stare. 'If you don't mind me saying so, you look knackered. Stay for a coffee.'

'Better be off. I'm on a hunt.' Uneasily she passed a hand over her hair. Certainly it could do with some attention, but not now.

She chose to walk and not drive to the street where Amanda Rivers lived. The girl had to be there this time.

She walked down the street. It was quiet and still, the rain had stopped but the pavements were wet. All the little houses turned a blank face to the street.

There was someone outside Dr Rivers' house when she got there, another woman. She was banging on the door, but she turned round as Charmian came up, and whether Charmian recognised her or not, Dolly Barstow knew whom she was looking at.

She stopped her onslaught on the door. The house looked even more neglected than when Charmian had been there before. Abandoned was the word, Charmian thought.

'No answer?' she said.

Dolly shook her head.

'Tried the hospital?'

'I came from there.'

Charmian went to the ground floor window and stared inside. The room had a dead, unchanging air to it as rooms do when they have been unused for some time.

'She's not there.'

There was a pause.

'I don't think she's anywhere,' said Dolly.

They stared at each other in understanding of the same dark truth.

They had started from different directions and had followed different paths but they had arrived at the same spot at the same time.

'My view too,' agreed Charmian. 'I think she's dead.'

Neither of them knew that on that day a farmer in Oxfordshire had discovered the remains of two bodies in a wood on a part of his farm which touched the Oxford to Banbury road. They were mere torsos and had been there some time.

Later that day, some wag asked: 'And were they suntanned?'

Chapter Nine

Windsor was a small town, a royal town, a town where rumours and tales spread on the wind. Someone once said it was like Cranford with a crown on. It was a town which usually had in it someone who knew more of the inside story than anyone else did, and in this case the person was Charmian.

She knew more of what was going on and said less. What she learned did not make her less fearful for Kate and Harry, but more.

Because of their involvement with Amanda Rivers, both Dolly Barstow and Charmian had to make statements to the officer in charge of the torso case, Chief Inspector T. Bossey. They did so, both of them, the day following the discovery of the bodies. Or what was left of them.

It was a chill, bright hard morning, more like a day on the east coast of Scotland where Charmian came from than the damp Thames Valley. But rain was predicted before evening.

Tom Bossey was polite, but he wanted to know what had been going on. In pursuit of that information he was prepared to be ruthless.

He was a man whose face had always the appearance of a gentle interested smile. Underneath he might be feeling quite different but you would never know. Charmian had been alerted by kind colleagues to this fact, so she knew what to expect.

'So?'

'No, nothing to do with the work that brings me here.' She found herself unexpectedly nervous. 'A personal interest. I am a friend of Mrs Cooper. Kate Cooper is my godchild.' Which you assuredly know already, she thought. 'Dr Rivers is . . . was a friend of Kate's. I thought she might know where Kate was.'

'At that time you had not suspected that Dr Rivers herself might have been the victim of violence?'

'I had begun to wonder . . . I suppose the clothes in the case that was found were hers?'

'It looks as though they might be.'

Clearly he was not a man who parted with any information easily. Their eyes met.

'Kate Cooper must have lent her the case for her holiday. Also the bathing suit.'

'I'm hoping to find that out,' said Tom Bossey. Far away and long ago there had been a French ancestor for Tom. He claimed descent from a French divine called Bossuet, and traces of that formidable man's genes could be held accountable for the hard strain in him. Or so he liked to think. His colleagues just said Tom could be a right bastard.

'So it was just chance, you and Barstow turning up on the doorstep at the same time?'

'Coincidence.' All the time she had been waiting with Dolly Barstow afterwards she had been uneasily aware that the girls were already assembling to have their likenesses taken. In the event they had gone off and had it done on their own, showing an initiative that she wondered at. What was Laraine up to? 'And you both realised at the same time that the house was empty?'

'Had been for far too long. I had been there once before.'

Looking for news of Kate. Which she still did not have. Where was Kate? Some place for which a case and clothes were not necessary. Or somewhere you did not know you were going. She just had to hope it was not a grave.

'I'd like to know where Kate Cooper is,' she said to Tom Bossey. 'I'm worried about her.'

'I think we all must be,' said Tom Bossey gravely.

'Has anyone checked whether the man Harry Jackson has or has ever had a house somewhere?'

To which he might have had a key, and to which Kate and Harry might have gone, or Kate alone, or Harry alone. There were those permutations to be considered.

Tom Bossey considered what she had to say, and answered obliquely. 'He is a violent man, and Miss Cooper in conjunction with him appears to show violence as well, but there seems no reason why these two, whether together or separately, should commit two violent murders.'

'We'll have to find them.'

'I think you can take it that we are now looking hard.' Then he added: 'Not only because Miss Cooper may have very important information about Dr Rivers that she ought to tell us, but for her own sake. Whoever the killer is, he or she may want to find Kate Cooper too.'

'You say she?'

'I am ruling nothing out. But we really know very little yet. It's all to do.' In fact, he knew less than he was letting her know. Time enough for that, he told himself.

Yet the discovery of the two bodies was no secret for long. With some speed a provisional identification was made of the female torso. From the age and the bony structure of the woman it looked as though it was Amanda Rivers. There were no helpful scars, but Amanda Rivers had borne no scars. Nor Kate for that matter. A young colleague from the hospital (not Len) came down to the mortuary to give a quick look, swallowed, shrugged, and said: 'Yes, it could be.' It had seemed best to let a medic have first look.

Her parents were informed of the finding of the body and the reason for thinking it might be their daughter. They lived in the South of France, but would be arriving as soon as possible. They had something to say. Amanda had gone on holiday with the man she expected to marry: Dr James Cook. Yes, she had certainly arrived in Rhodes, they had had a postcard. When she had not arrived back at the expected time they had thought she was staying on, although it was unprofessional and unlike Amanda. Yes, they had been worried, and of course they were apprehensive. But not of death, not of murder, not of this.

Dr Cook's partner had a look at the other body. He didn't

107

know what to say, but muttered an acceptance that it looked like Jim, but it was hard to tell and he was no expert. No, James Cook had no close kin.

To a question he said: Yes, he certainly had wondered what Jim was up to, the locum had been tearing her hair to get on to the next job, but he had been perplexed, wondering what to do, not wanting to harm Jim's career, he was a fine doctor. One more day and he would have informed the police.

'He wouldn't have,' said the young policeman taking the statement. 'Too cagey. He was waiting for things to happen without him having to do anything.'

Long before formal identifications could be made, everyone was saying the bodies could be matched to the missing limbs and that it was possible that they belonged to two doctors, lovers and fellow workers. These two people had been missing without anyone realising the significance of their absence.

They had flown out of Heathrow together, stayed in the same hotel, enjoyed their holiday, caught the correct flight home, landed at Heathrow and never been seen again.

Somewhere between Heathrow and Slough it looked as though they had died, and their limbs and bodies dispersed.

Dolly Barstow's interview took place much later than Charmian's. This was due to her own arrangement. She had considerable powers of procrastination, learnt at the large and powerful comprehensive she had attended, and she really had to have a word with Len Lennard before letting that pig Bossey talk to her.

She sat there, looking at his gently amused features and wondering what the genes had to do with it or if he was just a freak of nature. She was one of the few in the local force whose education allowed her to know who his ancestor Bossuet was. Yes, it was possible that the tutor to the Dauphin had fallen into some affair at the court of Louis XIV and thus permitted his blood line to get through to the next generation. Even for a bishop it must have been extremely difficult to remain a virgin in those social circles.

If you managed to hold on to thoughts like that, why you could deal with Tom Bossey more bravely.

'You were doing what exactly, Detective Barstow?' The smiling face did not alter, possibly could not, the structure of the bones not permitting it, but his tone was tough. 'Not a friend of Dr Rivers, were you?'

'No.'

'Nor of Kate Cooper's?'

'Never met her.'

'So what took you down there?'

'I was off duty,' said Dolly cautiously.

'A little private investigation?'

'I suppose you could call it that.'

He remained silent. Silence was something he was good at, so that to break it you found yourself hurrying into speech.

'I had an idea about the kidnapped babies,' said Dolly boldly. It was all right for her to say this. 'Just don't mention me,' Len had ordered.

'Come on then. Out with it.'

'The missing babies had been breast fed, but there did not seem to be any likely female suspect.'

He seized on the word. 'You're not suggesting a man could breast feed?'

'No, of course not, although when I was researching I found there is work going on to help men bear a child.' She enjoyed saying that, it was just the sort of concept to appal Tom Bossey. 'Nourishing the foetus on the stomach wall,' she added with pleasure.

'Oh, so you did research, did you?'

Dolly nodded, so she had. In her own way. 'I discovered, what I hadn't known, but it is apparently an accepted medical practice, that you can induce a flow of breast milk in a woman who hasn't had a child. I thought you had to have been pregnant and given birth, but it seems the glands can be stimulated by massage and such to produce milk.'

Silence again.

'So you see it would considerably widen the field of women to consider. But it would only be begun on a doctor's advice and in special circumstances.'

Tom Bossey looked as though he was glad to hear it.

'I was looking for the doctor. I had a list of names and I was working through it.'

'So your arrival there had no connection with severed limbs? You were not investigating that, privately or otherwise?'

'No. It was just a coincidence.' Then she added, even more bravely, 'But I still think I would like to see Dr Rivers' list of patients.' And her case notes, but they belonged to the Health Authority, didn't they, and would probably need an Act of Parliament to be unveiled. But there were ways.

'I will pass on your suggestion,' said Tom Bossey.

With surprise, Dolly Barstow realised she was being praised.

Through the agency of Dolly and Dr Len Lennard the news spread smartly throughout one segment of Windsor society. The hospital could talk about nothing else.

Within twenty-four hours the news was everywhere.

Charmian, whether she desired to be or not, was a disseminator of news. Because of her it was going to spread through Wellington Yard from Anny and Jack to Jerome and from him to Elspeth (who was back at work looking pale and tired) and from her to the wholemeal breadmaker and round the corner to the Robertsons, whose boy was better, but not willing to say very much yet. He was thinking about it and would tell his mother if he remembered anything new. It was all part of his illness now and he didn't care to dwell on it; besides, he had only seen her back and all he could say was that she was old but not very old. That could mean anything, as Bessie pointed out. 'He thinks I'm pre-war and I'm not forty yet.'

There was relief, mixed with an undercurrent of something deeper and less pleasant, in the Coopers' household. Charmian had told them what she knew of the bodies and their identity at the end of a long and unpleasant day. Until then she had managed to avoid Anny and Jack. But they

110

had to know. So she told them on her way up to bed.

'Not our Kate,' said Jack.

'It could never have been,' said Anny quickly.

'You weren't so sure.'

'In my heart I knew she was too sensible to get mixed up with anything like that.'

'Do you think there's a choice? Do you think that other poor girl wanted to die by violence?'

'It's a question of character.'

'Or your stars?'

'Yes,' said Anny seriously. 'Something like that. I see now that wherever Kate is, she is in control. That's what she is, someone who stays in charge.'

'Her godmother is worried. She doesn't say so but I can tell she is.'

'It's a professional preoccupation with her,' said Anny angrily. 'You and Charmian talk together too much these days.'

'I haven't said a word to her for days.'

'But you claim to know what she thinks.'

'She's worried about Kate, of course she is. I'm worried. So are you if you'd admit it.'

'Kate is not dead,' said Anny in a loud voice so that Charmian upstairs in bed heard it.

'No, she is not dead, but where the hell is she? And what has her part been in all this?'

'So we are back to thinking Kate a murderer, are we? I won't believe her capable of that.'

'Since she has known that man I have not known what she is capable of,' said Jack quietly. 'There is such a thing as "folie à deux", you know.'

Upstairs Charmian was thinking much the same. Muff sat on her bed and looked at her with a gentle gaze. Silence and contentment spread around Muff: she had the person she loved best, on whom she depended for all comfort and company, safe by her side, so she was happy. She moved to a better position on Charmian's arm so that she could anchor her victim more

111

certainly and began a confident purr.

'Push over, cat,' said Charmian, but in such a soft and loving voice that Muff felt no real threat. 'Why did I ever get into this business, Muff? Why did I come here? Well, I know the answer to that one. Ambition. I thought it would be that major step forward my career needed at this stage. And after all, what else have I got, puss?' She put aside all thoughts of Humphrey and whatever he might represent and that other man to whom she felt strangely drawn. 'And so it may yet, puss, so it may if I pull it off and I mean to, my dear.' Her hand went out to stroke the cat's soft head. 'But what am I going to do about this other business? The one that comes so close to Kate? I seem to have blundered into that one. What shall I do about it, because I have an idea, puss, just something I have seen.'

Muff purred louder. She, at any rate, knew how to behave and what to do. No problem: you simply made yourself comfortable and let yourself be happy.

'Not seen in life, puss, if you understand me, but with what my grandmother used to call my mind's eye. Three criminal processes going on in this town at the same time: the stolen babies, the murders, and the enterprise in which my Gang of Girls is engaged. I see that there is a loose connection between the first two, puss. I am going to seek out Dolly Barstow. She was looking for Dr Rivers, and I want to know more about that. Might be a link there.' She was getting more and more drowsy. 'Perhaps link is too tight a word, something looser, more casual, but somehow, somewhere there is a point where those two crimes touch, and at that point is Kate, so Kate must be found. . . . The other affair is a different case, though, puss. That must be quite apart.'

And she turned over in bed and went to sleep. Muff, dislodged, gave a gentle protest, and sorted out a good spot on the pillow where she breathed gently into her mistress's face.

Charmian, exhausted, had gone to bed early, but the girls were still up and around. They were meeting in Betty and

Elsie's flat, because it was nice and central, Laraine had said. What she did not say was that she did not want them at her place. Their group photograph was being passed from hand to hand.

'I'm glad we had it done. Even though she didn't come.' Everyone knew who 'she' was, you didn't have to name Charmian. Yvonne studied it happily. 'I've never had it done before.'

'The police do one for you,' said Nix.

'Oh well, that's different.'

'I'll say it is; I looked like an escaped lunatic. Not that I'm much better in this. Laraine's come out the best.'

'I've always been photogenic.' Laraine was studying the picture. 'Still, I'm not sure if we did right. Wonder why she really wants it?'

Yvonne looked surprised. 'Like she said: for her thesis.'

If you believe that you'll believe anything. But she did not say this aloud because to do this might provoke other doubts that she did not want to arouse.

'I wonder how this other business will affect us?' she went on.

'Nothing to do with us,' said Nix.

'I never said it was, did I? But it means more pigs hanging around the place. I don't like it.'

Nix shrugged. 'Give them something else to think about. Keep their minds off us.'

Laraine looked pleased. 'Good girl, Nix. You're right.' She got up and seized the wine bottle. 'Let's all have a drop more.'

Yvonne broke in: 'I thought they were meant to see us.'

'You'll be the death of me, 'Von,' said Nix.

'But if they don't see us, what are we doing?'

Becky said: 'There's some truth in that.'

Laraine put down the wine carefully, already a tiny stain marked her pleated silk shirt. 'Only at the right time,' she said, regretting, and not for the first time, the crew she was stuck with and who were so vital to her plan. Yvonne more than anyone.

Yvonne tried her patience once again. 'What a group we are,' she said with an admiring look at their photograph.

'We're not a group.' Laraine reacted swiftly. She would not be a group with that lot, she was different.

'We are a group,' said Yvonne with simplicity. 'Look at us. You can see it in our faces. They match. We're a set,' she added dreamily.

Laraine turned the photograph on its face as if she was putting the cover over a birdcage.

She was angry with Yvonne, she was angry with the photograph, and she didn't trust that policewoman Daniels. Who was using whom?

'Anyone seen Baby lately?'

'She hasn't been around,' murmured Nix. 'Why?'

Laraine shrugged. 'Just asked. Seemed a question worth asking. Is she part of your matching set, Yvonne?'

'She's not in the picture, so she can't be. She's different.'

'She's as clever as a wagon-load of monkeys,' said Laraine. 'I know that.'

Baby looked so small and delicate, so innocent that you forgot how sharp she was. No one better at looking after herself. Any hint of trouble and she disappeared. The ground kind of opened up and swallowed her.

'Have another drink.' Laraine went round with the bottle, pouring with a careful hand. Nix could take any amount without showing it except for a glitter in the eye. Betty was a sponge, but Elsie and Rebecca had to be watched. Yvonne usually went to sleep.

'Now let's get down to business. Nix, did you do the shopping?'

'Yes.'

'And you got the large size?'

'Jumbo. They don't come any bigger. Feed an army, I should think. Had to go to London, though.'

Probably safer, thought Laraine. 'And you paid cash?'

'Sure. And I've got the receipt to prove it.'

114

Laraine held out her hand: J. Doubleday and Co., Oxford St: one thermos flask.

'Good. Things in hand with you, Elsie?'

Elsie nodded. 'If that's what you call it. I'll manage what you want. Fancy a rehearsal?'

Laraine drew her lips in tightly. 'No thanks.' She was a squeamish woman and would not face certain things till she had to. A lot of people were sick at the sight of blood, she told herself. 'Leave it.'

'Suit yourself.' Elsie smiled, she had no blood sickness.

Nix broke in. 'What I want to know is: when do we get the invitation?'

Laraine looked at Yvonne. 'Well?'

Yvonne was vague. 'I dunno. I have to wait. Be patient. It's manners.'

'But we will get it?' Laraine tried to keep the tension out of her voice. It was terrible to be dependent on a half-wit like Yvonne. God, if they fell down on this point . . .

'Oh yes. I can see she means to give it.'

'But do we have to wait? Do we have to have it? Not like Buckingham Palace, is it?' Nix was impatient.

'You won't get in without,' said Yvonne, with what seemed like pride.

Nix drew in an irritated breath and started to say something. 'Yvonne, drat you . . . '

Laraine moved in to cool it. 'Don't push. Leave it. She's doing her best.' Which she hoped was true, but a badgered Yvonne grew stupid and sullen and worse than useless.

The party broke up soon after this. Laraine had acquired a small car and was obliging about ferrying around those who required it. Perhaps she felt safer if she had personally taken them where she knew they ought to be. Not that she was distrustful exactly, but she felt a check was wise.

Other checks were being run too. A quiet watcher in a car outside saw the departures. Laraine first with Nix and Yvonne,

115

leaving Becky to go on foot. After all, for her it was just around the corner.

A quiet almost tender surveillance was being kept on them; they must not be alarmed. The man on duty tonight reported to Harold English: Charmian had never met him although he knew her by sight and a fair amount about her. Since she was indirectly responsible for causing him a deal of extra work, his feelings towards her were not always friendly. They were not friendly now. It was late, it was raining again, and anyway chill for the time of year, and he was tired.

'Going to be a wet Ascot,' he said. 'Bet you.'

There was no one around to take the bet, but it was one way of voiding irritation. Ascot was about ten days away and he would almost certainly be on duty owing to Charmian. Since he liked a race, his wife liked to dress up and he knew a horse he fancied, he regretted he would not be there at the meeting. Or not as a spectator.

'That Daniels woman better be right.'

Just one more job for an overworked Force.

At this point Laraine got into her car, shut the door on Nix and Yvonne and drove off, forcing him to decide whether to follow her or Becky. He followed Laraine.

Her car was moving fast. A nippy driver, he decided as he followed discreetly, and not one he would trust to be careful. As he drove he thought.

No more babies had gone missing, that was good. He knew some mothers who never let their infants out of their sight. In his opinion they were wise and if more mothers were like them there would be less work in the end for people like him. He had a son of six months himself, he had instructed his wife to be on the alert. With weirdos you could never tell.

But they still had a double murderer to track down, and although he himself was not involved with this case, the extra work washed over everyone and he was due for leave in Ascot week. He could just see that going. Trust his luck.

He ran over the pattern of events. First they had had the

116

limbs, then it had been a hunt. They had got the cases, then the rest of the bodies. The process of establishing the identities had to be got under way. And they were looking for Kate Cooper.

One hunt had ended and another begun.

Chapter Ten

Charmian Daniels said: 'I want to see Amanda Rivers' body.'

A Windsor summer Sunday. A blue sky littered here and there with a few white clouds, the bells ringing, and the Royal Standard flying over the Castle. All quiet movement and light. Not so many tourists, the shops closed, and people going to church.

Charmian went to morning service in St George's Chapel and listened to the choir sing a radiant anthem by Bach. No Majesty present, she was worshipping elsewhere, but there was a Cabinet Minister and a new young Admiral. Molly Oriel was there wearing a new hat of a brilliant violet.

Now she was pacing the Long Walk with Harold English who had his dog, a large spaniel, with him. This was his excuse to be out, otherwise Sunday morning was sacred to domestic routine. Mrs English had her rules, after all.

'I want to see her body,' she said again.

'Is that really necessary?' There was a shade of distaste in Harold English's voice. No, something stronger, a deep reluctance showed itself.

'I need to.' I want to see her face. But she was not going to say that to him.

'I suppose it can be arranged.'

'I know it can be.' She could push when she wanted to.

'Will a photograph do?' Even that seemed to be more than he wanted to offer.

'No.'

'It will have to be under the rose,' he grumbled. 'Tom Bossey won't like it.'

'Oh come on. I'll just go and look. You need not be there. Or if there, need not speak.'

118

This meeting between them had been prearranged. One of their carefully casual meetings. The secrecy was the ruling of Humphrey who conducted his life according to a set of silent rules in which the left hand was not allowed to know what the right hand was doing. Unnecessary, Charmian sometimes thought, but she obeyed. It was his game, after all. She was only one of the players, probably did not know all the team, either. Nor they her.

They walked in silence with the dog racing back and forth barking wildly. Not as well trained as he could be, thought Charmian, surprised that a dog belonging to Harold English should be out of control.

'The kid's dog,' he said, half apologetically. 'Just lent to me for the walk.'

The dog came and jumped up at her face, breathing heavily. He smelt of old meat.

'What's his name?' Charmian pushed the dog away with a firm hand. He was like a young donkey. Goodness, she preferred cats.

'Teddy.'

Teddy circled them and sped off into the distance where he could be seen molesting another dog.

Harold English watched him with a frown. 'Have you wondered why they talk to you? Your lot, I mean. Wondered why they bother?'

'Yes, of course.' She fixed her eyes on the horizon into which Teddy was rapidly disappearing. 'Be a fool not to. But I think I know why. It's vanity. They like to talk about themselves. They're flattered by my interest.'

'I should think they'd mind.'

'I've told them they won't be named in any thesis. Or I wouldn't use their real names. But I think they'd like it if they were. No one's ever been so interested in them.'

'Not what I've heard.'

'Oh they've had lovers and enemies. But this is different. Makes them feel special. They always knew they were, now they think I know it too.'

119

'You're more cynical than I thought.'

'No, not cynical.' Charmian was surprised. 'Just how it is. And, of course, they think they are being clever. Cleverer than me.'

'And are they?'

'I hope not.' She was thoughtful. 'Laraine might be being so. I'm watching it.' She still had her eyes on the distance. 'You know, you're going to lose that dog.'

'I think so.' He didn't seem worried.

'Won't your child mind?'

'Be relieved, I think.' He remained straight-faced.

Charmian laughed. At last a touch of humour in the English family.

Then she went back to the subject in hand. 'There is no reason to believe either Laraine or Nix has access to guns or to explosives of any sort?'

'We think that Delaney may have passed a gun to Laraine. We have a photoshot of him handing something over.' He added carefully: 'That's new information. She made the contact with Delaney yesterday evening before going to a meeting with her friends.'

Charmian considered. 'She can probably use it, too. She had a boyfriend who was in the SAS. They stayed together for almost a year, which is a long time for her, she must have been attached to him. I think she may have picked up quite a lot from him.'

'Did she tell you this?'

'Not her. No, I found it out for myself. His name came up in the court records of her last conviction. I dug around.'

'Where is he now?'

'Took a job abroad. Oman, I think. He's out of this.'

'I think we can take it she's armed, and knows what to do with it,' said Harold English.

'She's dangerous all right, but I can't quite see the picture. They'd never get a shot in. Laraine must know that. No, it has

120

to be something else. Anyway, I don't see the others helping with a shooting.'

'If they knew what was going on.'

'That's true. They don't know.' Or not all Laraine could tell them. She was sure of that if she was sure of anything. Laraine was manipulating them all. 'In some ways they are a nice lot, and not killers.'

'You like them,' he said accusingly.

She shook her head. 'We have a complicated relationship based on a balance of suspicion and trust. I prefer to think that I see them as they are.'

'We could take them all in.' He had wanted this for some time. 'Find an excuse. Just till danger time is over.'

It might come to that, she could see, there was just so much security you could risk, and Laraine was pushing against the limits.

But if they did that then she would feel that she had failed the Girls somehow, let them down. Even Baby, who had initiated action by talking to Charmian in a rare burst of public spirit (or enlightened self-interest), wanted her friends protected. She had got that across.

Baby was still keeping a low profile, but Charmian was almost sure she had caught sight of her in the congregation at St George's, singing vigorously and wearing a new hat. Baby's prayers would be worth listening to.

'If we knew for sure when danger time was.'

'If we knew that, we'd be home,' he said. 'That's what you've got to work on. When. When. When.'

'I have an idea. Give me a bit longer,' she said. 'Just a bit.' She owed them that.

She was surprised to find this loyalty coming out in her so strong.

'There's one other thing,' he said. 'Laraine went shopping and was seen buying clothes for a cruise. Or anyway, a hot climate.'

121

'I don't know what to make of that. It says travel. Unless she's hoping for a hot summer.'

'You could try asking her.'

'I'm not supposed to know, am I?'

He did not answer this accurate taunt directly, having something else on his mind. 'There's something I ought to tell you: there's a built-in time factor to deal with. Delaney bought two tickets for Martinique via New York for June 23.'

Charmian said: 'Could be a trick to deceive us.'

'Yes. It could be.'

'It's interesting,' said Charmian.

'He's a swine,' said Harold English. 'Whatever he's up to, you can count on that.'

In the distance, the dog appeared, travelling at speed. He arrived and circled round them, barking enthusiastically.

'You haven't lost him.'

'No such luck. Home it is then.'

'When can I see the body?'

'Are you sure you really want to?'

'I am sure.'

Still reluctant, he said: 'I'll fix it for tomorrow. Early. You can get it over.' That was how he thought of it: an unpleasant experience that she need not have gone in for. He really did not approve of women police officers and unconsciously showed it. But it seemed as if there was something more than this. He went on talking as if his mind was on something else. 'Well, one other thing. There is no real sign of the Cooper and Jackson pair. Any sightings that were reported have turned out to be nothing. And Jackson does not own a house that we know of, the family house was taken over by his former wife when the marriage collapsed. He had lodgings in Uxbridge, still does have, the rent is paid up for the next month.' English paused, bending down to put the dog on the lead. 'But he did once own a kind of shack on Loch Tay, in Perthshire. His ex-wife let it out – there's no love lost there, by the way. He may still have a key. She thinks so and I'd say she was a good judge. I'm not saying they are there, but it's an idea.'

'Is anyone going to look?'

'The local police, of course. But it's pretty remote. On the edge of a forestry plantation. If they wanted to be elusive they could do it.'

Charmian was thoughtful. 'Any reason, apart from what the wife says, to think they might have gone there?'

'Well, a pair that fits their description did travel as far as Dundee on a long distance coach.'

'Thanks for telling me.' She decided not to tell Jack and Anny. Travelling by coach did not sound like her idea of Kate. 'What happened after Dundee?'

Harold English shrugged. 'Plenty of buses. Even a train. They could go on.'

'Or they might just be a couple returning home after a visit to London.'

She did not know what to make of the story, it did not seem as if he placed much reliance on it himself.

He shrugged and sighed. 'Now you're being difficult.'

'The pair I think I know aren't the sort to travel on a coach.' And she wasn't sure she put much weight on the ex-wife's tale, it might just be casual, hopeful malice. 'I'd like to be sure they are both still alive.'

There was a silence between them. Finally, he said, 'You're not thinking that you'll see the Cooper girl's face on the mortuary table and not Dr Rivers'?'

Charmian did not answer.

'It is, isn't it?'

'Yes. I want to see her face.'

'Then there's something I have to tell you. There is no head.'

Charmian stared at him.

'The bodies were headless.'

With too much on her mind, Charmian walked back to Wellington Yard. All around it was peaceful; nutritious and traditional Sunday lunches were cooking. Smells of roasting beef and simmering cauliflower floated on the air. Molly Oriel

123

had asked her to lunch so she was sure of a good meal.

If she could eat it. At the moment, her appetite was minimal. Harold English's news had sickened her.

'I'm a hardened police officer,' she told herself, 'but I cannot deal with death. Not when it comes so close.' She was going to keep out of the way of Anny and Jack for the moment, she was emotionally involved, and could be of no help to them.

It was too early to arrive at the Oriels' lunch party so she continued her walk. Anywhere would do. Down the slope of the hill, there was an art gallery which was having a private view of the work of a clutch of Thames Valley artists. Anny had had an invitation, but anyone was welcome. She would look in.

But on the way there, she saw someone she knew. Her 'contact'. But she had long since thought of him as a lot more than that, although she was still surprised it should be him.

He seemed pleased to see her. But then he usually was. Perhaps it was just his professional manner. She did wonder, sometimes. Easy to be with, hard to know. Probably he could say the same of her. It might be why they seemed to find each other attractive.

'Hello,' she said. 'Got your usual companion, I see.'

Jerome looked down at the pram he was pushing. 'I'm just taking him for a walk. One way of keeping the little beggar quiet.' His tone was fond. 'Elspeth offered but she's a bit broody about her own family prospects, and I thought better not. He's on the fidget today and he's usually so good.'

'Is he teething?' Charmian looked at the child who was asleep. In the way of young children he looked vulnerable and more babyish than his two years in his sleep.

'No,' said Jerome seriously. 'It can't be that. He has all the teeth he should have for his age.'

'Does he always do things by the book?'

'He's sort of average. Top average. But very advanced mentally, of course. And he's usually such a little man.'

'Oh I do love you, Jerome, only you could say that.' She was

124

sure the child was clever, though, but in some ways strange. Just as Jerome looked younger than the years she knew he had (that mop of curly blond hair did it), so his child often looked older, as if they were rushing to meet at some central point. You could not say that of many parents and children, usually they were moving apart at speed. Charmian herself had left her own mother behind years ago; her father had stayed closer for longer, but even he had dropped out of the running by now. It was the same with the Coopers and Kate, they loved each other but there was a deep divide.

Jerome looked surprised but pleased. 'Nice to be loved.'

'Oh, everyone loves you, Jerome.'

'That was what I was afraid of. Generalised love doesn't count. I want something more particular.' Then he looked down at his son. 'Still, if that little codger loves me, then I've got that.'

'Oh you have.'

They continued together down the slope. Even on a Sunday the tourist invasion had started. An hour or two later than in the week, but now in full flood.

'It's a responsibility,' said Jerome seriously. 'Who would he have if anything happens to me? I've made his grandparents his guardians and taken out some insurance. You have to think about it. Can't leave a mess behind. I mean if you go, that is.' He looked at Charmian. 'You ought to know all about that.'

'In my job? Yes, I suppose we see more of the mess that can be left than most. As you know yourself. I can never think of you as a policeman, Jerome.'

'I believed in justice.'

'Not law and order?'

'No, and it was when I discovered that they weren't the same thing that I left. No, it wasn't for me. Taught me a lot, though. How to remember faces, for one thing. For instance, although you don't know, I had seen you before.'

'Had you? When?'

'On a course at Northolt. You were giving a talk on crowd

125

control. You were good. You wouldn't see me, but I saw you. You had your hair done differently. It suits you better this way, may I say. Yes, you've changed, but I never forget a face,' he said with some pride.

'Hence your information you were able to pass on.'

'Oh that. Yes. Not much to that, but when I kept seeing Finch and Hooper around so much, I thought, Here, here, this wants watching. I knew them, you see, of old.'

'They know you?'

'Don't think so, although you can never be sure. I saw them both come up in court, Hooper and Finch.'

'On what charge?' Charmian ran over the various crimes for which Nix and Laraine had gone down. She could not think of one in which they had stood in the dock together.

'Oh, they beat up some man they said had been molesting Finch. I don't know what the truth of it was, except that they didn't like him and were prepared to do something about it. But they got away with it, because in the end the man didn't really stand up as a witness. Ashamed, I reckon, because they'd really done him over.'

'You don't like them, do you?'

'No,' said Jerome. 'No, I'd like to see them get what they deserve.'

'Funny you should see them.'

'All having a cup of tea together in The Brown Teapot next door to Woolworth's. I went in to buy some shortbread and there they all were. Didn't see me. Wouldn't have known me or cared if they had, I don't suppose.'

It was true, Charmian thought, Jerome could be the invisible man when he liked.

'What a witches' coven, I thought,' he continued. 'And that started me thinking.'

'I came into it because of a friend of mine,' said Charmian, thinking of Baby. 'Lines of communication do cross, don't they?'

'Yes.' Jerome accepted the idea seriously. 'It can be quite dangerous, sometimes.'

126

Charmian looked at the clock on the tower. It was time to go to Molly Oriel's lunch party. 'I must hurry.' She would have to give the picture gallery a miss.

'I'll push on.' Jerome gave his pram an energetic shove. The child stirred and wailed. Jerome cast a mock-despairing look at Charmian and walked on.

She watched him for a moment, touched by his devotion to his child. Sometimes he made her feel cheap, and selfish and mean, all of which she believed she was, but could usually manage to overlook.

He turned and saw her watching. 'Tell you what,' he called out. 'Come and have a meal one evening. At home with me, can't leave the kid, but I'm a good cook. Do a cassoulet.'

'Love it,' she called back. Then she went to lunch with Molly Oriel who was very bright and talkative, and Charmian found herself being bright and talkative back, discussing clothes with Molly, wine with her husband, and the prospects for Ascot with her neighbour, who appeared to have strong views on the subject.

But all the time, she was thinking: No head, no head.

'How very small they look without head or limbs.' She turned away from the metal tray drawn out for her inspection.

'They always look smaller.'

Perhaps the dead always did. Or the white-coated mortuary assistant was being deliberately matter of fact. No doubt he had seen all shades of emotion on inspections such as this and did not care for any of them.

'You can close the door now.'

The great drawer slid forward in the refrigerated cave and a door slammed shut on it. One more put away for the night.

It was always night in that room, with no windows and always shadowless artificial light.

'Seen all you want?'

'Yes, thank you.'

127

Seen enough to know that the quick recognition that it was or was not Kate wasn't going to come. Seen enough to know she was not going to tell Anny of what she had seen.

Outside she met the young policewoman, Dolly Barstow.

'Oh, Miss Daniels, nice to see you again,' said Dolly as if it was a surprise. 'You've been in to have a look?'

'Yes.' She had the strong impression that Dolly had been hanging about waiting for her. 'You too?'

'Yesterday. Felt I had to. Not any good, is it?'

'Not as a means of identification, no.'

'Silly thing is, I felt I'd know. Be able to say, Oh yes, that is Dr Amanda Rivers. But I couldn't. Didn't feel a thing.'

'I thought the same. And I've had a lot more experience than you. Ought to have known better.'

Dolly shifted from one foot to another, betraying an unease not usual in her confident young life. 'I heard you were coming in.'

'Word does get around.' So much for her visit being 'under the rose'.

'I've been told to go down to Amanda Rivers' house and make an inventory.'

Charmian raised an eyebrow.

'Oh, of course, it's been looked over, photographed and all that. But I'm to look at her personal things, women's stuff, that kind of thing.'

'Are you meant to be looking for anything specially?'

Dolly looked doubtful. 'I don't think so. Just notice what I can, I think. I wondered if you'd come down with me? Be a help if you would.'

Charmian said nothing.

'I know I shouldn't ask,' said Dolly apologetically. 'Better forget it, eh?'

'No. I'd like to come. I was just surprised, that's all.' She hesitated. 'This would be just between us, I suppose?'

'Well, yes,' admitted Dolly honestly, 'but if you did come up with something really important I think I'd have to say.' She produced some keys. 'Shall we go?'

'You're probably safe there. I don't think I've had an important thought for weeks.'

'Not what I hear,' said Dolly, giving her a sideways look. 'I've heard that you see things very sharp all the time.' Another quick look. 'I know what you're doing, of course.'

'I suppose you all do.'

'No.' Dolly was clear on that. 'I'm just good at catching on to things.'

Charmian did not believe her but she let it go.

'I wouldn't mind doing a research degree myself,' went on Dolly, as if that was all there was to it. 'Later on, of course. I've got an ordinary degree. I'm career entry, you see, speeded promotion, and all that. But everything helps if you want to get to the top.'

'And you do?'

'Yes.' A simple answer, short and clear. That seemed to be Dolly's style.

'I expect you'll do it.' Charmian was impressed by Dolly. 'Depending where the top is.'

'Yes, I've thought about that,' said Dolly seriously. 'For a woman the goals shift a bit. The goalposts too, for that matter.'

They had arrived at the house. Dolly let them in, closing the door carefully behind her. 'The neighbours watch all the time. Not that it's been much help. Or was much help.'

The house smelt stale and dead, as if it had taken a gulp of air some time ago and never expelled it. As a living organism, it was dead.

Dolly nodded. 'Does stink a bit. There was a mass of dirty laundry and rotting fruit and veg around. Don't think Dr Rivers was much of a housewife.'

'I suppose that's all the smell is?'

'I think they've had a look around for blood. No blood.'

They went over the house. Dolly was right: Amanda Rivers had been a casual housekeeper. But not a dirty one. Her books might lie about on floor and chairs, while her clothes lay

129

scattered around her bedroom as if she had just walked out, but everything was clean.

The house must just be one of those houses that build up a smell of their own over the years, picking up a bit from every past inhabitant.

In the bedroom, Charmian said: 'I haven't been much use to you.' She looked around her. 'She had nice things.'

'Fat lot of good it did her.'

'We don't know that for sure.'

'Agreed. But she certainly isn't around. And she didn't mean to stay away. I mean not for so long. She meant to come back on time from that holiday. That's how I read the house.'

Charmian sat down on the bed.

'I see she stores her dirty laundry in a black plastic bag.' There was such a bag filled with towels and underclothes by the window.

'Takes it to a laundrette in one, I expect. I do it myself. I buy blue sacks, seem more cheerful somehow.'

'Black bags are very common.' Charmian was still looking at the sack.

'There's a pile of them in the kitchen,' said Dolly. She added carefully: 'A lot of people keep a few.'

'Let's just go and have a look.'

The smell in the house seemed stronger as they went down the narrow staircase.

'I don't think the drains in this house work too well,' said Dolly. 'The lav doesn't flush properly.'

Charmian could see that the kitchen had been thoroughly searched and everything put back, but nothing in quite the right place. There was an old-fashioned coke furnace which looked as though it had seen good service. She went to the kitchen window and looked out, the usual sort of little garden. She stared out, thinking.

'There are more ways than one of identifying the bodies, of sorting out who they are.' Heads, faces weren't so important. Useful, though. 'Have they got the blood groups yet?'

130

'I believe so. Both group A.'

As was a large percentage of the population. Including Harry.

She turned and went up the stairs to the bathroom, and flushed the lavatory. It did drain away exceedingly slowly. She walked back down the stairs to the kitchen and ran the water in the sink. This seemed to run away normally, but there was a smell as upstairs. You couldn't say that the smell came from either source. It was just there.

Dolly watched in silence.

Charmian turned to her. 'Let's take a look in the garden.'

Together they unbolted the back door, turned the lock and went into the little back yard. An area of flagstones led to a tiny patch of grass with a few rose bushes. Dr Rivers hadn't been a gardener either.

In one corner was a manhole cover over a drain. The two women looked at each other.

'Let's get that up,' said Charmian. Without a word, Dolly went back into the house and returned with a big steel poker from the boiler. By means of it they levered up the drain cover.

In the bright sunlight they could see down the shaft which was neither very big nor very deep. At the bottom they could see a black plastic sack. From the drain rose a smell that was sweet and thick and sickening.

As Charmian turned away, she said: 'Might be a good idea to tell your colleagues to have another look at the bathroom.'

Chapter Eleven

After all, Charmian had to tell Anny and Jack what she had wanted to keep from them. There comes a point when you can't keep things to yourself, when it would be wrong to try. She had reached that point.

'No heads. There were no heads in those plastic bags. Just scraps of bone and tissue and blood. There had been quantities of blood.'

It looked as though the bodies had been cut up in the bath, in the drain of which had been found traces of body tissues and fat, particles of bone and blood. More traces had been discovered in the lavatory drain and in the kitchen outlet. Anything not disposed of that way had been dumped in bags directly down the manhole.

The other two took the news calmly. Perhaps they were not unmoved inside but they did not make a fuss. Charmian was glad about this quietness because she was very tired. It was the end of a long, hard day.

They were sitting in the kitchen of the Coopers' house at the big round table which Anny had designed herself and they had just eaten supper. Anny had taken one look at Charmian's face when she arrived at their door and insisted she stay to eat.

'Eat before you say anything. It's bad news of a sort, I can tell, without you opening your mouth. We'd all be the better for a meal inside us.' In spite of her brave words, she then looked at Charmian. 'I presume it is not news of an absolutely final sort?'

Charmian shook her head silently.

'No, I thought not. We would have had a policeman in uniform down here if it had been that.' She took a deep breath, it had to be with relief. 'Jack, get up a bottle of the good claret. It'll do us good.' A change of mood had come over both Jack and Anny. It was as if they had accepted something.

A piece of spiced ham and a great pot of beans baked with tomatoes, rum and black treacle appeared from the oven. One of Anny's famous meals for crisis times, the recipe was the legacy of a visit to an artists' colony near Boston. Had the Founding Fathers really added rum to their baked beans or was this Anny's own special contribution to the dish?

To her own surprise Charmian ate with appetite, and saw the others doing the same. But they ate with speed. They needed to get on to the talking.

'Saw you in the Chapel yesterday. I wanted to talk to you, but you went off so quickly.'

Anny was clearing away the plates and putting out some cheese.

'Yes, I wanted to walk.'

Anny gave her a sceptical look. More to it than that, her eyes said, don't think I don't know.

'Jack, pour out some more wine. We could all do with some. So you had a look at the bodies in the morgue this morning? I wanted to take a look, did you know that?'

'No, Anny, you kept that from me.' Deliberately, no doubt.

'And from me, too,' said Jack sourly.

'It seemed to me a legitimate request. I have an interest, after all. It might have been Kate.'

Charmian looked at her friend. Anny was calmer and more cheerful than for some days past. 'But you don't think so.'

Anny sipped some wine. 'I had a pang when you told me there were no heads. That churned me up a bit. Bound to. For the moment.'

'Have you heard from Kate?' Charmian demanded. 'Another telephone call?'

Jack said: 'Anny thinks she knows where Kate is.'

'I remembered something about that first telephone call. For a bit I thought it might be from a railway station. Then I thought maybe from a hospital. . . . Now I'm sure it was from an air terminal. As I look back there was that special quality to

133

the sound. I made Jack drive out to Heathrow and phone me to test it.'

'She did too,' said Jack.

'And it was like, very like. They were flying out somewhere. Or Kate was.' There was an intense look on Anny's face; she had made up her mind. 'She is abroad. I don't know exactly where but she doesn't know about all that has been going on here and when she does she will come back.'

It was another version of Harold English's story of the couple in Scotland.

'And that makes you feel better?' asked Charmian, who vividly recalled the message Kate had left: You will see Harry again. Or a bit of him. The bit I let go.

A nightmare picture of what Kate might be flying out with shot into her mind. Was it one head or two?

'You're not convinced?' said Jack. 'Don't know that I am myself really. The old girl goes up and down. First one theory, then another. Swings and roundabouts.'

'Shut up,' said Anny fiercely. 'I know, I tell you.'

Charmian looked down at her hands. To her horror they were shaking slightly. 'No one really knows yet who these two dead people are. Eventually, by working on the blood groups, which can be infinitely refined down and subdivided, it may be possible to tell who they are not.' Not Kate and Harry, she hoped. 'Even, possibly, if the hospital has some specimens from Amanda Rivers and Jim Cook and I gather they have because they were both cooperating in a survey testing a new drug, there may be a good guess at who they are. It may not be absolutely necessary to have the heads. But that time has not yet come.'

'Are the heads at the house? Or at the farm where the cases were found? Has anyone looked?'

Charmian had stopped her hands shaking by holding them together. 'I know that there was a very thorough search of the farm early on. I understand that another search is going on now. But as far as I know, although there were traces of blood on the farm, there was not much, not enough to suggest that either the killing or the cutting up was done there.'

'And the house?'

'That's being done now. We'll have to wait.' She thought that they would find plenty of evidence of blood there. Her bet was the bathroom, but it might be that scullery place behind the kitchen. There was a kind of murder and blood feel to that house. She shivered, although it was warm in Anny's place.

'You look exhausted.' Jack showed his sympathy in a practical way by pouring out some more claret. He did not usually waste either drink or sympathy on Charmian. She was not one of his favourite people. He had a pretty shrewd idea how she judged him, and in reply would say he didn't care for women police officers. But in his heart he knew that he was more than a little jealous of her. There was a bond between her and Anny that even marriage could not match. Nothing sexual, he knew his Anny better than that, Charmian too probably, and, anyway, he would have known how to deal with that, but something just as strong and deeper in their lives. You had to call it friendship but it was a weak word for a powerful thing.

'A day that starts with a visit to the morgue is not my ideal way of beginning the day's work.'

'What did you do after that then?'

'Oh I got on with work of my own,' she said vaguely. In fact, she had spent some time in pointless pursuit of Miss Macy, the patroness of the handicapped children, who had proved elusive. Not in her little house, nor in the charity shop where she helped in the morning. But the charity shop produced the information that Miss Macy had gone with a cousin to a gardening show but would be back tomorrow. Charmian would see her then.

Baby too had been hard to track down. Definitely in hiding, which was both interesting and alarming. Afterwards, she had had a searching session with her supervisor, who could, she had discovered, be uncommonly tough. 'That was in the morning. Then in the afternoon I went to London to talk about my next job.'

135

Anny looked surprised. 'I thought you'd be working here for a bit.'

'There's a time limit on that,' said Charmian.

'Oh?' Anny gave her a searching look.

'I only had a sabbatical term. It's coming to an end,' she explained. 'Of course, I'll continue in my own time. Finish it. If I can.'

'You don't sound too sure.'

'I don't think I'm a scholar.' No, she definitely was not, but she would go on with this, if she could. She owed that much to the group whatever happened to them. Nothing nice was coming, that was sure.

'I'd like to go on living here, though.'

Anny looked pleased. 'Sure. I'll do some more to the flat, if you're really going to settle.'

'You've done enough. It's lovely. No really, Anny.' She got to her feet, feeling heavy. 'I must go. Thanks for the meal. That was lovely too.'

Anny came with her to the door. 'Is the job in London a good one?'

'It will mean promotion. If all goes well.'

'You've never put a foot wrong in your career.'

'Is that what you believe?' Charmian laughed, but without humour. 'Well, I can think of plenty that could go wrong now.'

'You don't seem too pleased with yourself. Is it Humphrey? No? Jerome then? You do like him?'

Charmian nodded.

'He's a bit of a wild card. You know he put his wife on a pedestal and looked up. That's always dangerous. I'm just saying.' She added: 'Of course, she did die tragically, just after the baby was born.'

'Jerome's years younger than I am.'

'As if that made any difference.'

Anny kissed Charmian's cheek and Charmian put her arm round Anny's shoulder. For a moment the two friends stood together.

136

'If I learn anything positive, one way or another, about Kate, I'll let you know, Anny. You shan't be kept waiting.'

'She's still alive, Char.'

'Sure.'

Charmian closed the door carefully behind her and went up the stairs to her own place.

Muff greeted her with enthusiasm. The day had been all too quiet for that creature's taste. Muff liked a little excitement and loving company. Also she was hungry. The food left out had been a delicate piece of cod, speedily eaten and digested.

She put her point of view in a long, carefully articulated sentence. Charmian stroked her head, then opened a tin of cat food. It was Muff's favoured brand and she accepted the dish put before her with a tiny chirrup delivered from the back of her throat. Both parties recognised this as a gesture of extreme politeness.

Charmian did not go to bed at once, although she was more tired than she had been for a long while. It had been a draining day, with undertones of horror that lingered with her.

Nor had she wanted Anny's words of warning about Jerome. She loved Anny, but she occasionally resented her. Anny could come on powerfully at times, and then she felt weak.

She undressed slowly, wandering around the flat thinking. It would be a good place to live, if she was going to live in Windsor at all. Easy to commute to London. There was even a train service from the splendid Victorian station built for the young Queen and her consort. She could walk from the station to Wellington Yard. No problem.

Muff called from the door. Bed, she suggested, in a peremptory yet persuasive voice.

'Coming, Muff.'

There were three investigations going on in Windsor at that time and her path had crossed with all three.

She had come across Dolly Barstow on the doorstep of Amanda Rivers' house when they were both looking for the

137

doctor for different reasons. Dolly Barstow had thought Dr Rivers might be able to help with the case of the missing babies. Charmian had hoped the young doctor might know something about Kate.

What they had found had been worse. At that point two investigations had crossed.

And then there was her own special enquiry, investigation or mission, call it what you like. From whence came the feeling that this too had its link?

Emotionally it was linked and the link came through people. Kate to Charmian. Kate to Amanda Rivers. Amanda Rivers to Dolly Barstow and to Charmian. Invisible threads stretching from person to person.

Muff summoned her to bed, and she went. Lying on her back, eyes closed, seeking sleep like a cure for an illness.

Suddenly she jerked away. She was remembering something Anny had said. She had talked of the 'first' telephone call from Kate as if she personally, and not only Jack, had taken another call.

Did that mean she had heard from Kate?

Chapter Twelve

Charmian was early visiting Anny next day. She was up and dressed, ready for work and on Anny's doorstep as the postman came into the Yard with the letters.

Anny opened the door in her dressing gown. Her hair was untidy but otherwise she seemed alert and cheerful. 'Oh, it's you. I'm just making some coffee. Come into the kitchen and have a cup.'

The postman had got to her door, and was handing her a clutch of letters. Without looking at them, she put them in her pocket. 'Open them later.'

'Any for me?' asked Charmian. The postman sorted through his bundle and handed her a couple. The one on top she recognised as being from her mother, and there was a card that looked like business underneath. She'd read them later. Her mother's missives were entertaining but never full of hot news. In the kitchen she accepted a mug of coffee.

'Just going to take some in to Jack.' Anny went to the door. 'He's in a bad way this morning, poor old soak. We shouldn't have left him with the claret. Always does him in.' She sounded loving, though, which was by no means always the case with Anny.

Charmian waited till she came back. 'Anny, have you had a telephone call from Kate? A recent one?'

'No.' But Anny did not meet her eyes. She turned away to pour some more coffee for herself. 'Not exactly.'

'What do you mean?'

'I had a telephone call and a woman's voice said: "Did the flowers come?" Then we were cut off. Or the line went dead. I think the call was from abroad.' Anny sounded quietly triumphant, as if she had made a prophecy and it had come true.

139

'And did the flowers come?'

'No, no flowers.'

'Anny, that could have been from anyone.' Privately, she wondered if Anny was making it up.

'I'm sure it was Kate because of the flowers. Yesterday was Kate's birthday. You'd forgotten but I hadn't. It was a tradition with us that Kate sent me flowers.'

Charmian knew this was true. Kate did send flowers.

'I'll know when the flowers come,' Anny went on. 'Red roses. Wine red, blood red, my favourite sort.'

'I don't think it counts as evidence that would stand up in court.'

'Oh of course, you would say that.' Anny turned away angrily. 'Oh all right. I'm not mad, and I'm not sure. Of course I'm not. But I'm hoping, I'm terribly much hoping.' She pulled at the handkerchief in her pocket and the letters fell to the ground.

Charmian bent to pick them up to give them to Anny. 'I'll be off,' she said uncomfortably.

On top of the little pile of letters was a card. Anny stared at it. 'Wait a minute. Look at this.'

On one side of the card was Anny's name and address. On the other was the slogan VIRGINIA'S FLOWERS, and underneath a handwritten message: 'We are holding a bunch of flowers for you. We tried to deliver yesterday but could get no reply. Will you call to collect or advise us when we can deliver?'

Charmian handed it back slowly. 'Don't you answer your door, Anny?'

'I was working and Jack was out.' She clutched at the card as if it was precious.

Charmian reached into her bag and drew out her own letters. She too had a card with a precisely similar statement. She held it out silently to Anny. 'I was out most of yesterday.'

'Did Kate ever send you flowers?'

'Once. Once before.' Charmian had taken her godchild, then

140

a first-year student, out to lunch and they had had a quarrel, nothing much, but Kate had sent flowers with an apology. Yes, Kate did send flowers.

'I think I'm jealous,' said Anny, but she sounded very happy. 'Believe now?'

Charmian seized both cards. 'I'm dressed, you're not. I'll get the flowers and bring them back to us.'

A right turn out of Wellington Yard, then a few paces past the Robertsons' shop (already open for the day) and another right turn to VIRGINIA'S FLOWERS.

She knew the shop but she had never been inside. For a moment she hesitated, looking into the large plate-glass window with VIRGINIA written across it in large golden letters. Pots of roses and carnations with a large flat bowl of violets decorated the window. The place looked expensive and beautiful. Virginia, whoever she was, obviously loved her shop.

Charmian pushed open the door and went in. The air smelt fresh and damp with a sweet overtone of growing things. There was no counter as such but a long white trestle table ran the length of the shop. Standing by it, with his hands in a tub of freesias and white cyclamen, was a young man. Underneath a flowing white overall he wore black silk jersey jeans, tapering to bare ankles with feet in black suede slippers. There was a golden bracelet around one ankle and a matching one around his right wrist. He turned a gentle friendly face towards Charmian.

'Virginia?' said Charmian doubtfully.

'No,' he smiled. 'I'm not Virginia. She's a chain. There's one in Richmond and another in Roehampton and the top shop in Sloane Avenue. I believe there was a Virginia once, but she's Mr Ramsey now. He owns us Virginians.' Mixing sexes seemed to come naturally to him. He took his hands out of the freesias, dried them, and turned towards Charmian. 'I'm Freddy. At your service.'

Silently Charmian presented the two cards.

'Ah, you've come to pick them up. Our van tried to deliver

141

them yesterday but in vain, so I popped the roses in the cool room and the cards in the post.'

'You've got some lovely flowers here.'

'Haven't we? You wait till you see your roses.' He disappeared through a louvred door at the back of the shop to reappear with two large bunches of roses, one deep red and the other a startling blue white.

Charmian gave a spontaneous exclamation of pleasure. 'What a beautiful white!'

'Yes, Iceflow they are called. Very new. The red are good too, aren't they? That true deep red, really royal.'

Blood red, royal red.

'Is there a card with them?'

'No.' Freddy was still smiling. 'You don't know who sent them? Lovely surprise for you.'

'I'd like to know who sent them. We both want to know. I mean we want to say thank you. Can you find out who sent them?'

'Well, I would if I could,' said Freddy. 'But the order was phoned down from head office and I know no more.'

'Could you ask them?'

'Well, I could. But I've never found them very helpful.'

'Please?'

He put his head on one side, lips curving in a rapt smile. 'For you, I will.'

'Thank you.' Charmian waited while he disappeared once again to the telephone. She could hear his voice in plaintive speech. The conversation went on for some minutes, with Freddy's voice punctuated by silences while he waited for a response. Perhaps a search of the records was going on. Presently he came back.

'I got a little bit from them but not as much as you want, I'm afraid. This time I don't think they were being difficult, which is what I sometimes suspect them of. That girl at the end of the phone is not a friend. But really I don't think they know more: they had a telephone call placing the order from abroad. It was done through the international "Flowers By Request" arrangement and was paid for by an American Express card.'

'Abroad? Where abroad?'

'Paris.'

He had really done quite well, got a lot of information. 'And the name of the sender?'

'Ah well, they weren't so helpful there. No message, you see, and they could hardly make out the name, the French chap not being great on English. Sounded like Roper.'

Or Cooper? So was it Kate?

'Thank you.' Charmian gave him her own special smile, reserved for nice helpful witnesses, and got his special smile back. Neither of them meant much by it. She gathered all the roses, red and white, to return to Wellington Yard.

Red roses, white roses. They probably were from Kate. But for what purpose? Kate remembering the birthday ritual? Or registering remorse for a deed done?

You could take it either way.

At the door she stopped suddenly, remembering something. 'Give me that pot of African violets. How much? Thank you.' She had a purpose for that pot of violets.

She carried the flowers back to Wellington Yard where she handed the roses over to Anny who was dressed now and had brushed her hair. 'Here, take these. Put mine, which I suppose are the white ones, in water for me and I'll collect them later.'

Anny took them. 'Well?' she asked.

'Yes, it looks as though the flowers came from Kate. It's a possibility anyway. The order came from Paris. No message but the sender's name sounded like Roper. It's just possible that it was Cooper. I expect it can be checked.'

'It means she's alive.'

'I don't know what it means. Not for sure. And neither do you. Don't depend too much on it, Anny. It could be someone playing tricks.'

Anny looked incredulous. 'No. Only Kate chose those roses in those colours. Has to be her. She is alive.'

Charmian cut across the celebration. 'Whatever you believe, you have to let the police investigating the murders know. Yes, you have to, Anny. Tom Bossey's the man. Inspector Tom Bossey. Ask for him.'

Carrying the pot of violets, she left.

She walked round the back of the Yard to the side road where she always parked her car. She was always mildly surprised it was still there each morning and unvandalised. She could think of some cities where this would not happen.

It was only a short drive to Miss Macy's house and this time the lady was at home. Charmian could see her in her front garden where she was doing some weeding. She sat for a moment studying both the house and its owner. It was the end house in one of the neat terraces of early Victorian houses that graced Windsor. Behind a white picket fence a narrow front garden led to a green front door with a bright brass knocker. Miss Macy matched her house. Queen Alexandria had probably been alive when she was born and would certainly have approved her discreet cotton dress and dark blue gardening apron worn with a big hat. The garden looked as though it got a lot of attention.

Charmian got out of the car, carrying her pot of violets. Her choice had been a wise one, the woman who lived in this house would appreciate violets.

Miss Macy straightened up as Charmian walked through the gate and up the narrow path. 'There's no parking out there, you know. Double yellow lines. But I suppose the police can do as they like.'

'You know who I am?'

'My girls told me. We saw you in the Park.'

Charmian was a little surprised, but not very. The observer had been the observed. It did happen. Nor was she surprised by the slight aggressiveness of the lady. She was true to her period, probably 1920s radical and long time feminist, with a small private income, and a feeling for good antiques co-existing with a feeling that you owed the world something. She would not

144

like the police force and was probably a founder member of all societies protecting the liberty of the individual from radical childbirth to euthanasia.

Charmian knew she would like her, respect her and find her maddening. 'In a way they are my girls too,' she observed mildly.

'Humph,' said Miss Macy. Charmian had never heard anyone achieve this sound before and she was momentarily diverted. Perhaps no one outside Windsor did say it any more. 'I question that.' And she gave Charmian a look of blue-eyed shrewdness from beneath the gardening hat. 'Is that pot plant for me?'

'Yes.' It no longer seemed such a good idea.

'A sweetener, eh? It's root bound, any fool can see that.' She held out a hand. 'Give it here.' She was tapping the base of the pot smartly as she spoke. 'Dry as a bone. Where did you buy it? No, don't tell me, it would only grieve me. I hate flower shops. Like keeping animals in a zoo.'

So she was into freedom for plants as well as women and animals.

'I'd like to talk to you.'

'Come into the house while I water this poor creature.' Miss Macy led the way inside.

Her house obviously received less attention than her garden. Although probably quite clean it was not well dusted and bore witness on every side to the variety of Miss Macy's interests. On a round library table was a quantity of children's books, old well-used books. Next to them stood a box full of toys. A strong smell of Plasticine arose from it, taking Charmian back immediately to her own nursery school days. So children still used Plasticine, did they? There were also about a dozen paintboxes, a pile of old newspapers, and on top of it several pairs of scissors. Children always wanted scissors. There was also a First Aid box. That covered the children. An easel leaning against a wall suggested that Miss Macy also went in for a bit of sketching from nature. She had a spinning wheel and a small loom tucked into a corner. These had a faintly neglected

145

look as if not a lot of attention had come their way lately.

Miss Macy saw her gaze. 'That tweed didn't work out,' she said. 'Wasted that lovely wool. Hair really, from a local goat farm.' She removed a copy or two of *Country Life* from a chair. 'Sit down while I water this plant.'

There was no obvious sign of her interest in women prisoners, but on the wall was a range of photographs of school groups and somewhere among them must be Yvonne. Charmian got up to have a look.

'Interested in those groups?' said Miss Macy as she returned, the violets now thoroughly wet, even sopping. 'All from St Joseph's Church of England School in Arthur Road. Still there, but you wouldn't know it. Gone comprehensive.' She made it sound like a disease. Perhaps it was. 'I taught for thirty odd years.' She planted the bowl of flowers firmly on the table, carefully mopping up any drops of water. She respected good furniture. 'Been out of it now for almost ten, thank goodness.'

'I want to talk to you about one of your old pupils.'

'I can't betray any confidences.'

'I like Yvonne myself,' observed Charmian gently. 'I'd like to help her. And, of course, the more I know about her the more I can help her.'

Miss Macy sat down heavily on a chair already bearing a large tabby cat. The cat made a reproachful sound but did no more than squeeze itself into a corner of the chair. 'Good boy,' said his mistress, patting his head, and then to Charmian: 'He's glad of a good home. One of the strays from the Park. There's always a colony there. This is one the foxes didn't get.'

'About Yvonne?'

'Yes, but you've seen her for yourself. She was a nice, gentle child, she's a nice gentle woman, but not very bright and without any strong moral sense, I'm afraid. And she's very easily led.'

'Not dangerous at all?'

'Only to herself. You know her record and what it amounts to.'

146

'She's learning to read and write better. She thinks that will help.'

'Thirty years too late,' said Miss Macy. 'But try if you like.'

'She's all right with the children, I suppose? You seem to trust her. All of them,' she added, after a pause.

Enthusiasm showed on Miss Macy's face. 'All the girls are absolutely splendid with my little protégés. It's a sign of grace.'

'You think so?'

'Oh yes, you should watch them some time. They are all so intent and careful. They have been the greatest help, a real boon. I have taken them on several outings now and they have never failed me. For women with their background that is something. Perseverance, sticking at things, is usually their greatest weakness. They can't hold to anything.'

Except what suits them, thought Charmian cynically.

'But they have been so reliable,' went on Miss Macy. 'Of course, there must be something in it for them, one knows that,' she continued. 'I am not foolish, too much is not to be expected from them.'

'Don't we know?'

'There are contradictions. Within their own group they are capable of great constancy and loyalty.'

'I had noticed.' She was thinking of Yvonne and Elsie, they were loyal. Baby also, in her way.

'But, of course, that loyalty can be played upon.'

'I had noticed that too.' She was thinking of Laraine, a manipulator if ever she had met one.

'Good.' Miss Macy lifted the cat from behind her and placed it on the floor. Without any hesitation it leapt back to where it had been before and settled down again. 'I don't know what I can tell you about Yvonne. You've met her, what she is now, she was as a child. Mild, polite but hard to read. You couldn't be sure what was going on behind that face. Not much, I suspect. I can't say I have been surprised at her subsequent career, poor woman.'

'No?'

'No.' She spoke with a detached sympathy that Charmian admired: she aimed for it herself. 'She never showed much understanding of mine and thine, what she fancied she liked to have. And once someone showed her the way . . . ' Miss Macy shrugged.

'And did someone show her the way?'

'Oh yes. An older girl at school took her shoplifting. And then Yvonne took her mother. Of course they got caught. Hopeless really.'

Yvonne's crimes, like Yvonne herself, seemed relatively harmless and easily punished. It was a pity, though.

Charmian expresed this view. 'A shame her marriage did not help her.'

'It did for a while. I had hopes, especially when the children were little. She was a good mother in her way. But they grew beyond her, and so did her husband, whereas Yvonne stayed where she was. Her husband gave her up in the end, although I believe he did try.'

'Thank you for telling me. I haven't got to the bottom of Yvonne, but you've helped.'

'Oh, you won't. Not with any of that group. But should you try? It's like playing God.'

'Unluckily, it's my job.' But she already knew that Miss Macy did not like policemen. It was a perfectly legitimate point of view.

'Help but don't ask them why, that's what I do. They are coming with me and a bunch of children from St Elfrida's Home on Ladies' Day to see the Queen and all the Royals get out of their cars in the Great Park (I know exactly the spot to sit, under the big oak), and into the carriages for the carriage procession down the Ascot course. We shall have a picnic and enjoy it.'

'When's that?' asked Charmian.

'Next week. But the big treat comes the week after, on the Monday, a real red-letter day with the Fête on the Thames which the Queen will attend. The Eton boys will row her barge.

148

It's a secret about the Queen coming, but I know she's going to be there. I shall take my little band.'

'When's that?'

'June 23,' said Miss Macy, looking at a wall calendar.

As Charmian left, she thought, That's valuable.

Miss Macy went back to her gardening. Interesting conversation, she said to herself. I suppose I told her enough and not too much.

She's pretty sharp, thought Charmian as she drove away. I hope I didn't let too much out.

Both had their reasons.

Charmian made a swift telephone call to the special number she had been given. Harold English answered her.

'I think the day is June 23,' she said. 'June 23.'

Later that day, after a full session of work, seeing her supervisor, who inspected her notes and suggested she have a group meeting with her subjects, and a note from Harold English with an interesting suggestion (which she would consider), she learnt through a talk with Dolly Barstow, who seemed to have an excellent intelligence service, that the woman, the remains of whose body had been found, had had a recent abortion.

That should help to sort things out. One by one the details were being assembled that were to establish the identities of the bodies.

Chapter Thirteen

At the end of such a day, the last thing she wanted was a talk with Jack and Anny, but it had to be, they were waiting for her at the foot of her stairs when she came home.

'You've heard.' With a sinking feeling she made it a statement, not a question. She was in for a long session, she recognised the signs, Jack white and aggressive, Anny tense. 'Come in, have a drink and let me feed Muff.'

Jack said: 'No way is that Kate. No, that settles it to my mind. Not Kate.'

In a remote, cold voice, Anny said: 'As far as that goes, it could be Kate. Take no notice of Jack, he does not understand these things. And if it had been her one could see why she was in such a state before she left. But it is not Kate because she sent me flowers. She is not dead.'

In London, where they had now arrived, Amanda Rivers' parents had said much the same thing, and Dolly Barstow had duly reported it. They don't think so, she said. 'We do not believe it can be our daughter.' Those were the exact words.

Parents rarely know their own children, Charmian thought, or what they are capable of, and one set or the other of them here were going to be in for a surprise.

A nasty surprise, this case was getting nastier by the day. There were three puzzles occupying her mind at the moment and elements of them seemed to seep like poison from one to the other, and the themes of death and birth and blood to transfer themselves from case to case. These cases might not be connected, but by God, they were related.

'Sooner or later,' she said to Anny, 'it will be discovered which of these two young women had an abortion. It'll come out.'

150

'If either,' said Jack.

'They are the prime candidates.'

'Oh you are hard,' said Anny.

'Am I?' She was tired, not wanting to talk, but to wash and change. Also to feed Muff. Tonight she was going to have her meal with Jerome. A cassoulet, he had said. She hadn't though of him as a cassoulet man, he had seemed to be more a steak and onions and carrots man. But whatever the dish, she was hungry and wanted it.

'I'm sorry, Anny. I've done the best I can. I just don't know about Kate. It seems to go this way and then the other. On balance, I think she is alive and that the dead woman is Amanda Rivers, but until we get a certain identification we can't be sure.' And even then they would not know where Kate was or even if she was alive – there was more than one way of dying.

'There's the man too,' said Jack suddenly. 'No one says much about him, but he's there.'

'They will be working on him. Something may emerge, must do so in the end. Just hang on, be patient. I know it's hard.'

'And Kate may come back any minute,' said Anny. 'She may come walking down the road, surprised at everything.'

'I shall have a word to say to her if she does,' said Jack grimly. And then: 'I wish the heads would turn up.'

'That may never happen,' said Charmian.

'What?'

She shrugged. She could think of any number of ways of disposing of heads, none of them nice to think about, but better not to tell Jack and Anny. Jack seemed to see reserve in her face.

'Is that all? Anything you know but aren't telling us?'

Yes, one thing but she would keep it to herself. Dolly Barstow said that the police had checked the arrival of the flight on which Amanda Rivers and her companion were alleged to have come from Rhodes. It had arrived late but without incident. Everyone had hung around for a while organising

151

taxis. There was a lot of use of the telephones. Rather sooner than most, a couple who could have been Amanda Rivers and Jim Cook had been seen getting into a car and driving off. The suggestion was that they had known their driver. None of the Heathrow taxi regulars had admitted to being the driver of that car.

To Tom Bossey this fitted in with the idea that the dead bodies were those of the two doctors. They had got into the taxi, driven off and ended up murdered. But Dolly did not see it that way. No, she said to Charmian, you could not count on that episode meaning anything at all. To her mind, the question of the identity was still wide open. Those two could still turn up alive. She'd been in love herself and done strange things. Missing work? Yes, even that, Dolly admitted sadly, although she wouldn't do it now.

Find the taxi driver, Tom Bossey ordered. Check on all recent abortions in this area and in London. It would take time.

Time. June 23, she thought.

'I'll keep you in touch,' she said to Anny and Jack. 'When I know anything positive you shall know it too. And you might do the same for me.' But she knew she might keep things from them, might be obliged to. They should not rely on her telling the truth. Perhaps they did not, they were not naive. 'Meanwhile, I'm going to have a hot bath.'

'I suppose you think better in a bath,' called Anny as she and Jack left.

'Yes, but I'm not going to. I'm going to lie still and be mindless. . . . And don't let the cat out.'

But Muff must have got out, because when Charmian hurried down the staircase on her way to Jerome's, there she was on the middle step, opening and shutting her mouth in silent displeasure.

'I'd take you with me if I could,' Charmian picked up the soft limp bundle of fur, 'but you were not asked.' She pushed Muff through her door. 'Food is in the dish in the usual place.'

The plants in the big pots at Jerome's door had developed

great heads of flowers and revealed themselves as a form of single geranium. The soil looked dry, though, as if a thorough watering would not come amiss.

Jerome greeted her warmly, and there was a comfortable smell of good cooking.

'Those big pots of yours are looking a bit dry,' she said.

He came out and gave them a look. 'Doing nicely, aren't they? Don't want to give them too much water, though. Might rot the roots. Geraniums like to be dry. Dry but well nourished. I think I've got it just right.' He was a gardener then, as well as nurse, cook, hairdresser and ex-policeman?

'How's the baby?'

'He seems well.' Jerome spoke with the grave pleasure he always showed when he discussed his child, as if he was talking about some splendid artefact for which he was responsible. 'His grandmother had him all today so I could get on with the cooking. I had to fight off Elspeth who likes to feel she is the only one except me entitled to handle him, but fortunately she is still off colour so she didn't put up much of a struggle.'

'Is her husband not home yet?'

'Coming soon. She had a telephone call. From Aberdeen, I think it was. Cheered her up a lot, she's better when she has something to look forward to.'

'Aren't we all?'

'Well, there's the cassoulet.'

He brought it to the table in a great brown casserole which Charmian recognised from the shape as one thrown by Anny. It was the classic recipe too, based on a goose. She was surprised. Half wondering if it might not have been a vegetarian cassoulet. But no, here was the genuine thing.

'And the goose? Where did you get the goose?'

'From my mother-in-law. She has a butcher's shop.'

'That's surprising for a woman.'

'She inherited it from her father. But it's not such a difficult trade to learn. A woman can do it. It's skill, knack.

153

Occasionally you need a bit of brute force. I help out at times.'

A woman can do anything, thought Charmian, as if you didn't know it already. Even chopping up a body. Only I don't want to believe it. Not of Kate.

You don't have to believe anything, a detached cold little voice said in her ear, speaking as from space, just keep your eyes open and use your brain. Something is being offered to you, see it. Life is stranger and darker than you suppose.

They ate the cassoulet, and the child slept and made no sound. Jerome went in and looked at him once, coming back with a smile. 'Sleeping.'

'Goodness, how you love him.'

Jerome smiled again, no words to express what he felt, but he touched her hand. 'You would too.'

There was no pudding, because cassoulet is a filling dish, but he had cheese and fruit to offer. Conversation was casual and easy, not touching on the murders, or the missing babies, or her study of the women recidivists.

It's domestic, thought Charmian. We are having an evening like any ordinary, normal family. But, of course, we can never be that. There is no real link between us. It's a make-believe. Nothing can come of it, except dashed hopes. I wouldn't even be a good mother.

'Can I fill your glass?'

Perhaps he interpreted the look on her face as thirst. 'Thanks, Jerome.' She held out her glass. 'I've learned to like wine, it took me a bit of time, I wasn't born to it, but now I do.' She sipped her wine, it was quite an ordinary red wine, nothing special, but it made her want to talk. 'I've got a problem. Harold English, who has no power over me professionally, in theory, but yes, probably has in practice, has come up with a suggestion. I don't want to follow it but I am going to have to. My supervisor thinks so.'

'And this is?'

'There is going to be a press and TV interview the day after

154

tomorrow on the torso case. Scene of the crime, pictures, a call for witnesses. The sort of thing TV does so well. It will go out live and also on radio. There will be an audience. Public invited. Tom Bossey who has set it up thinks he will get a big response. Perhaps the breakthrough.'

'Get a lot of publicity, anyway.'

'He's not averse to that either.'

'And the suggestion is?'

'That I take the Girls, Laraine and Co. This is so that as many police officers as possible see their faces without the Girls knowing they are being looked at. Harold English seems to think this is a good idea.'

'He's a cold man,' said Jerome thoughtfully. 'But clever. Out for number one. And do you think it a good idea?'

Charmian shrugged. 'I accept it.'

'But will they come?'

'I think they might. For some reason they are anxious to oblige me.' Or Laraine was, and the others followed her lead.

'Well, it's interesting.' He poured himself some more wine and laughed as he drank. 'Fancy old Bossey coming up with the idea of audience participation. He's another one. Always grinding his own axe. I might look in myself if I can get a sitter. Just tell me where and when.'

Charmian let her hand rest on the table. 'Do you think you'll stay in Wellington Yard?'

He thought about it. 'No. Probably not.'

'You're worth something more.'

'You think so? That's nice. But it's more a question of time and place. This is right for me now.'

His hand was on the table, their fingers touched. Charmian looked at him. Jerome was so many things, as well as an ex-policeman he was a loving father, a shop-keeper, occasional car hire driver, and amateur hairdresser, that she found him hard to sum up, but she was always aware of the strong virility behind the gentle manner.

'Yes,' he said. 'Very much yes.'

155

'Well?'

'But it's the child, you see. Not with the child here.'

Charmian moved her hand fractionally back. 'I suppose that's not my style either.' But all the same, she felt rebuffed.

Chapter Fourteen

On the next day, while Charmian went about her unexceptionable business, two encounters took place.

Young Robertson, convalescent from his nasty attack of chicken-pox, told to seek fresh air, but bored with his own company, strolled down Peascod Street. He had had plenty of time to think during his days in bed, and he had diverted his mind with thoughts about the mystery of the bodies. His moment of fame had come with his story of the black sack on Dr Cook's doorstep and the woman looking at it. People had listened to him, asked him questions and taken him seriously. But now events had bypassed him. Or so he felt. Perhaps they no longer believed he had seen anything.

'Don't believe me,' he told himself, as he walked around Marks and Spencer's. 'Think I'm just a kid,' he said as he bought chocolates in Woolworth's. 'But there was a woman and a sack and I did see her,' he announced as he entered Boots the Chemists for a look at their computers. He was a keen student of computers and meant to have his own one day. And that day was not going to be far off if he had anything to do with it.

Because he lived in a shop which sold newspapers he knew all the details of the torso murder mystery and of the cases of the missing babies. His family had a personal interest here. Details about the importance of the breastfeeding of the infants had filtered through to the shop where they had been keenly discussed by Mrs Robertson. He had listened, marvelling at the way grown-ups went on, also at their dullness of perception. They only seemed to see what they thought was there, a boy saw what was really there.

From personal observation he had decided that there was more in the arrival of Charmian Daniels than met the eye. He did not approve of women police officers, they should leave it to men, but he recognised that they had their place. They could look after women and babies. Female children preferably. Leave the men and boys alone. So he had concluded that Charmian had really come here to investigate the missing babies. It was a proper thing for her to be doing, and he would have a word with her about this when he was able, because on this subject also he thought he knew something. Not much, but something.

He wandered out into Peascod Street and decided to take a look at Wellington Yard before going home. He liked the Yard, always had, even in the days when it had been derelict and before Jerome and all the others had moved in. He had played there, pretending to be a horse in the old stables. Anny and Jack and now Charmian lived on that spot.

As he turned down the hill towards the Yard he saw a familiar figure ahead of him looking in a shop window. Something about the stance and the clothes reminded him of the person he had seen staring at a black plastic sack outside Dr Cook's.

So that's who it was, he thought. He hurried his pace. 'Hello,' he said.

'Hello, Brian,' she said.

'Peter,' he said. 'I'm Peter.' She was only interested in babies, not really in boys. He had noticed, having felt the cold touch of indifference before.

In the Armitage Clinic in West London a young woman doctor was talking anxiously to a colleague.

'I know it was her. She came in under another name, but it was her.'

'You could be mistaken.'

'I'm not. We were at college together. I haven't seen her since, but still . . . '

'We are supposed to be absolutely confidential and discreet here. It's one of the things we charge for.'

158

'I know that.' They were both part owners, together with two other doctors, of the clinic.

'If you got it wrong, it could be bloody embarrassing. She wasn't on your list, I hope?'

'Adam Farmer got his assistant to do it. She was only six weeks on so it was a breeze. She was out the same evening.'

'Have we had a direct enquiry from the police?'

The young woman looked towards the desk where their receptionist was at the telephone. 'Minna says we have. A constable called. She put him off, but he'll be back.'

'I should keep out of it, if I were you. You're only guessing after all.'

She had made her decision. 'No, it can't be done. It's murder, after all, and it could be important evidence. I have to say.'

Chapter Fifteen

Nothing in Charmian's life had prepared her for the writing of her thesis. She was glad to leave it behind for today's outing. It was still early days but she was labouring. As a student she had written essays, as a police officer she had made careful notes from which she had then compiled a report. But it was no preparation for what she was doing now. She had written an outline of her first chapter: Character and Background, she called it, but filling in the outline felt like writing a novel. She hoped it wouldn't read like one, but whoever heard of a novel with footnotes?

Even done in a straightforward way, character by character from Laraine and Nix through to Yvonne, there was no denying she had her favourites. She liked Nix, feared Laraine and was sorry for Yvonne. About Baby, Andrea as she must try to call her, she mercifully did not have to write since she was not included in the group.

It was meant to be factual, dispassionate, the work of a scholar. Well, she wasn't one, it was becoming tiresomely clear. She would write her thesis, it would be presented in due course, she had promised that to herself, but it would never be accepted. Humphrey would have been proved right: she should have chosen some other cover.

If it was a cover. Laraine for one was showing more and more scepticism. She was sitting next to Charmian now, on one of those hard official chairs, looking quietly pleased with herself. Another new suit too, Charmian noticed. Pale blue linen with a dark blue shirt, and big pearls with matching earrings. False, she presumed, unless Laraine had robbed either a bank or a jeweller's. Hadn't she been seen staring into a jeweller's shop? There had been a report of that surely?

160

'When does the show begin?' she murmured to Charmian. 'I thought coppers were supposed to believe in being punctual.'

'Here they are now.'

The Chief Constable, a Chief Superintendent whom Charmian knew by sight, and Tom Bossey filed in. A supporting cast of lesser characters came in behind, to assist those who had already been sitting waiting like the rest of the audience. 'And they are on time.'

'Only because of the television crews,' said Laraine. 'I suppose they'd go on overtime if they were kept waiting.' She seemed interested and excited in spite of her words. 'Some familiar faces in that lot that just came in.' She sounded amused.

They were in the front row where they could be seen easily and Charmian had arranged her group in order as suggested by Harold English. Nix and Laraine on her left, then the others on her right. As expected, they had made no fuss about coming. The idea had amused Laraine as she knew it would.

No trouble about getting leave from their jobs, either. It was becoming increasingly clear to Charmian that they did not expect to be staying in them much longer.

She had brought them in as a group, again following Harold English's suggestion, and she had felt like a mother hen with a group of strange birds.

Jerome was sitting two rows behind and slightly to her left. But she was very conscious of his presence. He had looked them over speculatively as they came in, getting a quick stare back from Laraine in return. Dark suit, curly hair brushed, he was at his best.

Another friend was sitting in the back row, almost out of sight. Baby, now to be called Andrea, wearing dark spectacles and a new hair style, possibly a wig, had put in a discreet appearance. Not surprising, but interesting.

The Chief Constable stood up, introduced himself and his colleagues and explained, in the lucid, polished manner that had got him his job, the purpose of the meeting, asked for the

161

help of all concerned in 'this terrible crime' and sat down.

Tom Bossey then took over. His manner was not polished; he threw the words at his audience as if he hated to part with them. But he got across what he had to say.

He went through the case from day one. He told of the finding of the limbs contained in the sack in Wellington Yard, then he moved on to the discovery of the cases on the farm out beyond Datchet. He even made a little joke which got a polite murmur, no more because you could tell he didn't think it funny himself but only put it in because a light touch was good lecturing style.

He recounted the finding of the torsos, minus their heads. Then on to the search of the house belonging to Dr Rivers in Charlton Street which had strongly suggested that the bodies had been cut up there. It was probable, he said, that the deaths had taken place in that house.

But they had problems. He listed them.

They did not know for sure who were the dead couple. They all knew who was missing, he did not have to tell them. Still, he did so. Dr Cook and Dr Rivers were well-loved local doctors, everyone must feel involved, he wanted help and he knew he would get it. That was what this was all about. Yes, questions could be allowed.

His audience, in which local ladies were well represented, drank in all those details which they might have missed or which might not have been available to them. Molly Oriel was there, taking notes, Charmian saw.

Blood groups? Yes, work was being done on this, but had not proved conclusive. Delicately, he brought in the matter of the signs of recent abortion on the female corpse.

This certainly was an area where he expected help. Someone had to come forward with information, because it was there in the records somewhere, someone knew, it had been a professional job.

Yes, they had officers going around to all likely clinics and hospitals but so far nothing definite had come out.

In time it would do, but publicity would help. He needed the assistance of both the TV and radio on this one, please.

Photographs of various scenes in the story appeared on a wall screen, and the television cameras at once took them up. There was Wellington Yard, the farm where the cases had been found, the ditch and the road leading to the farm and finally the inside of the house in Charlton Street.

No pictures of the torsos, it was not that sort of a show and if anyone present had been hoping for a quick horror then they were disappointed. Charmian looked at her watch; she knew the strict timetable would be kept to which meant that all would be over in a few minutes.

From the back of the room an elderly woman stood up and asked about the kidnapped babies. Was there any progress? Did the police see a connection?

'Not my case,' said Tom Bossey smartly, 'but I understand we are satisfied there is no connection. The investigation is proceeding. But I can offer no more answers.'

Laraine sniggered. 'I bet not.'

Dolly Barstow looked at Charmian across the room, and shrugged her shoulders.

There could be one link anyway, Charmian thought, and that could be Amanda Rivers. Bossey knew this and was probably lying.

Nix said: 'This lot couldn't kipper a herring. But I could fancy that one in the white shirt with big stripes.' This was the Chief Superintendent. 'A brute but tasty.'

'You always like a bit of the rough stuff,' said Laraine contemptuously. 'You can keep the lot of them. Scratch a policeman and you'll find a killer.'

'Oh rubbish,' said Charmian.

'Some of the time, not all of the time.'

'You do go on,' said Nix tolerantly. 'We all know you hate policemen.'

She hates all men, thought Charmian, but not nearly as much as she hates herself.

163

'I can look around me now and see at least two that are capable of it. One I know about, oh he did it strictly legal and in the way of duty, I believe he got a medal.' That made it the Chief Constable, but it was years ago. 'And as for the other,' she shrugged. 'Maybe he's done it. I wouldn't know.'

There was a final explosion of questions with microphones thrust under Tom Bossey's nose from all sides, and then it was over. Equipment was rolled up and there was a rush for the stairs.

'And who's that then?' demanded Charmian as they started to file out. She caught Jerome's eye and smiled at him. She didn't want him to think she was any different after what had happened. Or hadn't happened.

Laraine looked at her slyly. 'Try guessing.'

Yes, she hates men, Charmian thought, and she hates herself and now she hates me.

Nix put her arm round Laraine's shoulder. 'Do as much bird as she's done and you'd be as daft as she is. That's a nice suit. Buy it for Ascot?'

Laraine pushed her arm away. 'Get off.' She began to walk away, colliding with Baby, also making one of her fast exits.

Charmian caught up with them. 'What did you mean in there? You can't just say things like that and get away with it. What am I to guess?'

'You don't know anything about people. You're really thick. Think you can understand us? Or anyone? How you ever caught anyone beats me. Don't you see anything, ever?'

'What do you see?'

'I tell you what I've seen. I've seen a man who killed a dog because it killed a cat.'

'I might do the same.' Or feel the same, but probably not do it.

'Then look for your match. I'm not saying any more. It's dangerous.'

Charmian grabbed Baby before she could escape. 'What was all that about?'

164

Baby looked vague. 'How should I know?'

'Talk to her. Try and find out, it could be important. I think she knows something.'

Baby hid behind her dark spectacles and said she would try. It was debatable whether she was more afraid of Charmian than she was of Laraine. If pushed too far, she would simply disappear.

Not beyond finding, because Baby had her little habits, her chosen places, which made her easy to locate, but it would take time and time was what Charmian guessed she did not have.

She had not seen Harold English at the meeting, but he had been there because now he was getting into his car. Jerome had disappeared. She walked away herself, wondering how many unobtrusive figures were following Laraine, Nix and Co.

Ascot week. Ladies' Day.

'Come to a drinks party and then we'll go to watch the changeover from the motor cars to the carriages. A lovely chance to see the Royals, the Queen is always at her best, her favourite day. I know just the place to sit.'

Molly Oriel had a pass – without one you did not get through the barrier. Charmian accepted her invitation. She knew it had been set up by Humphrey, Molly Oriel was just putting a good social gloss on it. As always.

It was a fine warm day with only a few clouds in a blue sky. Hours before the arrival of the royal cars the grass under the big trees was crowded with cheerful groups in summer dresses.

Molly Oriel had brought a picnic and champagne, but after a little while, Charmian loosened herself from the party and wandered away. Molly watched her go, speculation in her eyes.

Wearing sunglasses and a soft hat with a brim, Charmian hoped to be unobtrusive if not unrecognisable. She had already marked down where Miss Macy, her group of children and her band of helpers had settled for their picnic. There they were on a couple of large rugs with thermos flasks of coffee for the adults and soft drinks for the youngsters. If Molly Oriel had

165

chosen a good spot to sit, this group had an even better one. A kindly policeman had helped to settle them right up against the protective rail so that 'they could get a good look with no one in front of the little 'uns.' Their party was on one side of the road down which the royal party would arrive and Charmian was on the other, but she had a clear view of them. She knew that closer to them would be other watchers.

There they were, Laraine and Nix, Elsie and Yvonne and Betty and Rebecca all dressed in their best and with their best faces on. Even Laraine could be seen handing a seated child a sandwich. From Slough, Datchet, Hounslow and Old Windsor, they had assembled.

Currying favour with Miss Macy so that they could be with her on the Big Day, June 23.

Well, it won't be a bomb, she thought, they have no explosives except themselves, or not yet, but Laraine has a gun. Not on her today, you couldn't hide a gun in that tight suit. She had a shoulder bag, though, but was paying no particular attention to it.

Perhaps after today they should take them all in. See what she got today, how they behaved, what she could make of it. Then a policy decision would be arrived at in which she would have a voice.

The open carriages into which the royal family and their guests would move had already arrived and were lined up under the trees. A splendid cavalcade of some half a dozen vehicles, some built in the reign of Victoria with the others dating from Edward VII and his son and successor, George V. Old as they were, these carriages were in magnificent repair, polished and full of colour, while on the horses every inch of rein and bridle was supple and soft, with the bits and decorative brasses shining like jewels. The coachmen of a piece, their caps and uniforms swagged and decorated with ancient imperial splendour. The elegance of the livery was in itself marvellous to see.

The coachmen, postillions and grooms were regulars, grown old in the royal service, familiar friends, always seen. 'I know

166

that man,' whispered Molly Oriel, coming up to her side, 'the one that looks like an illustration by Phiz. He's always here. Known him for years. As long as I've been coming. And that one, and the man behind.' She was smiling at them, giving little waves of welcome but not a flicker of expression marked any face in return. Training held. Even the horses, beautiful greys, remained still and calm.

'Must be a great bore for them,' said Charmian absently, her eyes still on the party across the road.

'Oh no, they love it. The annual Ascot visit is a kind of picnic. All sorts of treats. The Queen is a frightfully good boss to work for.'

Molly ought to know, living as she did in the shadow of the Crown. It was becoming harder to see across the road, the carriages were drawn up on that side, nearer to Miss Macy's outfit who were thus blocked from her view. She separated herself from Molly, moving to a better spot.

It was getting hotter now, with the sun overhead, striking brightly through the trees. The scene on the grass, full of animation and gaiety, was like an open air party. Very English, thought Charmian, still the Scot, like Henley or Glyndebourne or the one Oxford Commemoration Ball at which she had been a guest. With Humphrey, of course. There was something about the summer air and grass that suited the English spirit.

The noise level was rising, on every side the sound of laughter and happy voices. The sound of a champagne cork, music from a radio, a child singing. People standing up, glass in hand, eyes beginning to turn hopefully towards the gate through which the Queen would come.

Everywhere was movement and life. Except, as she suddenly observed, with Laraine and her allies. They were still, quiet, concentrated.

She started to move, her legs were carrying her across the road towards them without her willing it. Not next week, she thought, but today. Whatever they are going to do, they are about to do now.

167

She was moving fast, weaving her way through the crowds. Even as she moved she was thinking: But they aren't killers, not even Laraine. Nix is wild, but not crazy.

At the end of the road the royal cars were in sight of the drawn-up line of carriages. There must be a noise, the sound of the cheering, but she could hear nothing. She was frozen into a band of silence that was moving with her.

And yet what did she see? Nothing so terrible. The women were standing close to the rail in a calm line, gazing at the first carriage. Rebecca and Betty side by side with Elsie and Yvonne a little apart. Laraine and Nix stood together and seemed to have nothing more alarming about them than a large thermos flask which was in Nix's hands.

She was almost up with them when the first royal car drew level to the carriage. The Queen stepped out, halting for a minute in the road while the rest of her party alighted. She looked happy and relaxed, talking to her companions. As always she stood out in a dress of pale lemon with a big lemon and white organza hat. It looked like organza anyway because although it was big with a large brim you could see her face through it clearly, and she was smiling.

The Queen started to get into the carriage where her seat would be about level with Nix and Laraine.

Nix was fiddling with the top of the thermos.

'That's a big thermos,' Charmian thought. It was very big indeed, about the biggest she had ever seen.

Nix had the top of the thermos off when Charmian began to run.

The Queen had turned her head towards where Molly Oriel stood. Molly was smiling decorously and making a bob. No doubt they knew each other.

Charmian got to Nix and Laraine just as Nix raised her arm to throw. Nix was shouting.

'Help for women prisoners. We are women too.'

The others were shouting too, echoing Nix's words. Not Laraine, she was just standing there with a slight smile on her

168

face. Doing nothing, saying nothing, but full of triumph.

Behind them stood Miss Macy, shocked and speechless. Charmian pushed past her, treading on a child, and grabbed Nix's arm.

She was surprised at the strength in Nix's arm and the fierce, angry look she turned upon her. A furious, non-seeing look that was focussed on some inner vision.

A great gush of blood spouted forward in a wide arc, leaving the thermos like a projectile. As it fell, drops spattered all round. Charmian got her share. So did Nix.

The carriage moved away smoothly, its wheels spattered with blood.

'Our blood is on you,' shouted Nix, 'we're giving it back.'

The Queen appeared not to have noticed. She was gone, driving smoothly away to Royal Ascot, with the rest of the procession falling in behind her.

Red blood, liquid blood, falling blood. It was amazing how potent it was as a symbol.

'You fool.' Charmian was hanging on to Nix, gripping her wrist. She hated the feel of the blood on her dress, the wetness of the blood on Nix's arm. 'You bloody fool.'

Nix laughed. 'Bloody, anyway.' She seemed to have recognised Charmian now. 'You got that right, anyway.'

Charmian did not let go. 'What the hell do you think you are doing?'

Nix laughed. 'Making a splash.'

All around them was a confusion of noise and movement. She was conscious of Rebecca and Elsie being taken away, of Yvonne crying. She could hear Miss Macy's voice, protesting. 'Not her fault,' she thought.

But Laraine was smiling.

'This achieved nothing,' Charmian said fiercely. 'Absolutely nothing.'

Laraine still smiled.

Rebecca Amos

169

Betty Dedman
Laraine Finch
Elsie Hogan
Nix Hooper
Yvonne King.

All of various addresses in Old Windsor, Datchet, Hounslow and Slough.

All in police custody for the night and due to appear in the magistrates' court the next morning.

She stood looking at them in the small interview room.

Let them stay, she thought. Let them stew. Especially Laraine. She felt sorry for Nix, who, as she saw now, had a real streak of fanaticism and was willing even to enjoy crucifying herself. She was a believer, you had to believe in something, she had said so herself. Rebecca and Elsie had been paid, Elsie for the cow's blood she had provided, that was what they believed in. Betty Dedman had taken her cut, as was her habit, and Yvonne had just been caught up, as was hers. It had been extremely unlucky for her that she had known Miss Macy, or she might not have been recruited. But unluck and Yvonne were old companions.

But Laraine? What moved Laraine, who did nothing without a purpose and that purpose the welfare of Laraine?

'I don't know what you think you've done, except make fools of yourselves.' And to a limited extent of her, too. 'Well, you're in here now and I'm afraid you'll stay.'

'Fine friend you turned out to be,' said Nix. 'But don't think I'm sorry. I'm glad I did what I did. Women should shout for women. I'll be in the history books.'

'Prison first.'

Laraine said with confidence, 'You won't keep me in. My lawyer will be round here any minute and I'll get bail and be out. Nothing to it, you'll see.'

'You'll stay here tonight.' And she left them to it.

In the corridor leading from the interview block and again in

170

the main police building she saw signs of intense activity. Harold English crossed her path as she made her way to the door. His face was sour.

'What's up?'

'We've been done. The Great Park caper was just a diversion. While we were concentrating on a group of lunatic women, Delaney and his pals were robbing a bank. Finch knew all right, knew what she was doing even if the others didn't. She was seen giving it the once-over. Premises in Upper Sheet Street.'

'Delaney?' Charmian was thinking of Laraine's joyful face. Yes, she had known all the time. That was what she had been up to. And escape to warmer climes with Delaney was what she had been smiling about. She didn't love him, but he was her ticket to ride. 'You'll get him. Stop him at Heathrow.'

English gave a short laugh. 'He's done us there too. He had another ticket booked. Just the one. He flew out to Brazil this afternoon. All on his own.'

They talked for some time but eventually Charmian left, not with any love for English in her heart. Pesky devil, she thought.

Outside the building, in the pale of a late summer evening she found Baby loitering while pretending to admire the view. Sorry, not Baby, but Andrea. Beryl Andrea Barker.

'Surprised to see you.' It was unlike Baby to put herself in a position of risk.

'Wanted to know what happened. Oh well, don't tell, I can guess, poor bitches. I feel I've betrayed them.'

Charmian shrugged.

'You did too, pretending to help them.'

'I can still do that.'

'Oh sure,' said Baby sceptically. 'Only will they believe it?'

'I was doing my job,' said Charmian. And earning a living and getting promotion. It had to be that way, it was the manner in which society worked.

Baby sighed. 'Women, see. It's a woman letting a woman down.'

171

'Not only women. I didn't let Laraine down, she did that to the rest of you. And now she's been let down. By a man.'

'What do you mean?'

'You'll find out. We've all been led up the garden path.'

Baby hesitated. 'Not the only reason I came. Wanted to tell you something. Remember you asked me to talk to Laraine? Find out what she meant with that remark of hers?'

'About policemen and murder? I remember.'

'I did and she told me.' For the first time Charmian realised that Baby liked her, was even fond of her, would do something for her that might cost. 'She said she'd seen him around Windsor, he lives here. And he'd seen her, she said. And she laughed. So I suppose you must have seen him too.'

One way and another that could cover quite a number of policemen.

'You going to walk home?' There was a taxi across the road.

'I'm not going your way,' said Baby. 'There's my bus. I'll just get on it.'

And she disappeared from Charmian's view, perhaps for ever.

With Baby you never knew.

Charmian walked slowly towards Peascod Street. She let herself linger, looking in the shop windows. She felt drained, stupid.

It had been a remarkable day, but not a pleasing one. Her legs felt heavy. Depression, that was what it was. She stopped in front of an antique shop. It had a Victorian cradle in the window, with a china-faced doll amid the lace and frills. Take some keeping up, a cradle like that, she thought. Not to mention the laundering of the long baby clothes. Layer upon layer of silk, cotton and wool. Just as well it was only a doll inside them.

Down the hill she fell in with Dolly Barstow, who was also staring into a shop window.

'Hello.' She joined her at the window and stared in herself. It was a chemist's shop, and they were looking at a display of pregnancy testing kits.

Dolly turned her head briefly. 'Quite a day.' Then she turned back towards the window. She did not say anything about the episode in the Great Park, although she undoubtedly was well informed.

'You can say that again. . . . Anything new about the torso case?'

'Yes.' Dolly gave a thoughtful nod. 'One thing. A woman doctor came forward with some info about the abortion. Pretty clear it was Amanda Rivers.'

'What we thought.' Anny would be relieved. 'Thanks for telling me.'

'Yes. Don't pass it on just yet. Her parents don't know.'

'So the heads don't matter?'

'No, the heads don't matter.' Dolly was still thoughtful. 'Glad to see you. I had a thought.'

Charmian looked around her. It was getting late, shops were closing, but there was a coffee shop still open and serving. 'Let's go in there.'

Once settled with a mug of black mocha each, Dolly was fluent. 'We've been working on the association of Rivers and Cook. Not just personal, though they'd known each other a long time, he'd been divorced, and she wasn't exactly virgin territory.'

'Dolly!'

'Oh well, yes, sorry, bad taste seeing she's probably dead. But we've been taking a sneaky look at their professional side too. . . . Records are confidential, but well, we've managed a quiet look. On the side, as it were, just to see if any motive for murder comes out of this. Been trying to find a connection. They have some patients in common, you'd expect that. A popular local doctor and an obstetrician and gynae specialist. He did a lot of pre-natal work, but he referred difficult cases to the hospital. She got some. That was her job. She also helped run the Fertility Clinic, took a special interest in it. Helped those who couldn't conceive and those who did it too readily.

173

There was that side to it as well. Emotional stuff.'

'Yes. So they had some patients in common? Such as?'

'Well, the Robertson family for one, although lack of fertility wasn't their problem, the other way round, he had a vasectomy that didn't work. They were upset for a bit.'

'They like the kid now though.'

'Oh sure.' Dolly hesitated. Then began again. 'You know the lead I was working on originally? It was part of the inquiry into the missing babies, I got drawn into the torso case through that one.'

Charmian nodded. 'So what?'

'Mulling it over, I've been wondering . . . Supposing there was this woman, couldn't have a child, but was going to get an adoption. A new baby. Angel in the house sort of woman. Felt she wanted to be a real mother, breast feeding, the lot. Rivers did have a couple she was leading that way. Speciality of hers. We've talked to one success in the art who now has a happy suckled baby. She doesn't want to be named, but she's in the clear. Supposing such a woman took to borrowing other people's babies to help her on the road?'

'Weird. Got a candidate?'

'One or two possibilities.' Dolly did not amplify.

'Are you tying it in with the murders? Not a motive for murder, surely?'

'Not a motive,' said Dolly. 'Not a motive exactly, but a link.'

The wheels were beginning to turn. Lists would be drawn up and worked over, checks would be made, the dull plod of police work would begin, and the sort of results you could offer to the Director of Public Prosecutions would roll in. The process had already started.

She gave the wheel a push. 'On the torso case . . . Laraine Finch, now in custody, claims to have a name. Might be worth following up.' The irony of it was not lost on her. Who was telling on whom?

'Oh yes, her. One of that lot.' Dolly acknowledged that which she had been carefully avoiding. 'I expect they'll get

174

Delaney. Meanwhile he has got over a million to stash away somewhere. They may never get that back. Will you go on with your thesis?'

'I'm going to try,' said Charmian.

Chapter Sixteen

For the next few days, Charmian took evasive action. Wellington Yard, Windsor itself, saw little of her. She was much in London making arrangements in connection with her new job. Chief Inspector Charmian Daniels would be raised to Superintendent with every hope of going even higher. She had a meeting with her new colleagues, not one of whom, she was glad to see, had she ever known before. She might enjoy working with them.

A pattern of life was set up that she adhered to during these days. She would return to Wellington Yard late at night, avoiding Anny and Jack and everyone in the Yard, as if she did not want to know them any more. And yet she would continue to live there if she could. In pursuance of this aim, she ordered the telephone to be put in her flat. It was installed quickly.

Once the telephone was in and calls being received, she dodged meetings with Tom Bossey and Harold English, and refused an invitation to lunch with Lady Oriel. Humphrey she saw constantly because she had to.

Some anonymous hand (she suspected Harold English) sent her a mass of newspaper cuttings about the Windsor Great Park affair: they were not as bad as she had feared. The Queen came out of it well, the police much less well. Charmian was not named. All the women, in spite of Laraine's optimism, had been remanded in custody. Not dangerous but loony, seemed to be the current view, so they were to be kept inside and observed. Miss Macy had gone away to stay with friends in Scotland, she was reported to be very distressed. As well she might be, thought Charmian.

As for the Torso Case, as the papers called the affair, she felt out of touch and was glad to be so. Temporarily anyway.

'Police search beauty spots in hunt for heads,' ran one headline on a paper caught up with the other cuttings. This item might have been put in on purpose. Harold English (if he was the sender) was by no means as straightforward a chap as he appeared to be.

Several days passed. A great band of heat stretched over southern England. The north was cloudy, Scotland wet, but in the south the temperature rose ever higher. A storm was predicted before evening.

In the afternoon she had an interview with her supervisor. Sitting over a cup of tea in the senior common room, deserted now for the Long Vacation, he suggested that her thesis would gain greatly in interest and depth by the chance to see her 'group' through this experience. They were to be let out on bail, except for Nix who had suffered a kind of breakdown and was in hospital, but they were among those she was avoiding. But they would have to be faced eventually, she owed it to them and to herself.

From this interview on the Tuesday, she returned not as late as usual to the Yard. The sky, heavy all day, was growing darker by the minute with uneasy flashes of lightning streaking the clouds. The Yard was still open and at work but there were lights on in the shops.

Dolly Barstow was one of the people who had got through on the telephone, to say that in the Torso Case she thought there were going to be developments. Ring back, she said, and learn more later. But when Charmian tried, once from London in the morning and then in the afternoon from a public call box on the university campus, she got no reply.

One more try when she got home, she thought. Muff first, then Dolly.

She bought a rye loaf at the baker's in Wellington Yard. The shop was empty except for a few loaves and a teabun.

'I must be one of your last customers.'

The woman behind the counter admitted to being hot and tired. 'Been a funny day. Thunder gives me a headache, and

177

then we've had the police in and out of the Yard all day, digging up some of the flagstones.' She lowered her voice: 'They've been asking us about the sacks we get some of our flour delivered in.' She looked harassed. 'Seems there was flour on the limbs.'

'I thought I saw something as I came in. What did they get? I'll take the teabun too.' There was a kind of sticky teabun with sultanas made only in the Yard to which Muff was particularly partial. If it was well buttered it often kept her quiet when catfood would not.

'They'll be back, I expect.' She sighed. 'That'll be another twenty-two pence.' The woman looked up at the ceiling uneasily. 'That's thunder again, getting closer, too. Well, I'm just closing up now and I'll be home with luck before the worst of the storm breaks. We're all a bit tense here with all that's been going on. I'm not the only one affected. Mrs Cooper looked downright ill and Jerome seemed in another world.'

Charmian turned back to her own staircase, hoping to avoid Anny who must be on the look-out for her. But all she saw there were empty, blank windows staring back at her blindly. Glancing up at her window she saw an angry tabby face glaring out. I've got you a teabun, she wanted to shout, you'll be happy with that, I have thought about you even if you don't believe so. Muff was always convinced she was doomed to be a lost, abandoned cat. Two minutes on her own and she knew you had gone for ever.

Charmian bumped into somebody, the bread and teabun went flying. 'Sorry, my fault.' She bent to pick up her purchases. 'Hello,' she straightened up. 'It's Elspeth, isn't it?' The woman looked flushed and unwell. 'Are you all right? I hope I didn't hurt you.'

'No.' Elspeth seemed on the point of tears. 'I'm all right.'

'You don't look it.' This was true – there were patches and blotches on her face, one of which had already risen into a crested spot. Others seemed to be on the point of erupting.

Elspeth turned her face away. 'I've got chicken-pox.'

178

Charmian stared at her, suddenly understanding the significance. 'Oh Elspeth . . . It's been you. . . . And you caught it from the Robertson baby.' Talk about poetic justice.

'I'm not going to talk about it. You wouldn't understand.' But I would, thought Charmian, of course I would. 'Jerome's given me my cards, and Mrs Robertson has rung the police and that's it.'

And Elspeth put her head down, and walked out of the Yard. Probably into the waiting arms of Dolly Barstow who would be well pleased with the acumen of her deductions. She was no doubt making preparations now for taking Elspeth in, which accounted for her not answering her telephone.

The first few heavy drops of rain were falling. Jerome had come out of his shop and was standing between his two great tubs of geraniums. He looked flushed and angry.

'Silly bitch,' he said.

'I never thought of Elspeth.'

'I did, but I couldn't believe it. And now she's brought the police down on us.' He did not sound admiring of his ex-colleagues, but then he never had been.

'They've been around before,' she reminded him.

'Not like this. She's admitted that it was her dragged the sack of legs round to the Yard and dumped them. The Robertson boy finally made up his mind it was her he saw.' There was fury in Jerome's voice. 'And guess why she did it? Because "the doctor had been so good to her", with advice about how to get an adoption and she couldn't bear him to be involved in anything nasty. She'd had a look inside the sacks, you see. Also she thought anything nasty for him might hold up her chances of adoption. So she hoisted the sack round here and dumped it on us.'

He was dragging at his big pots of flowers as if venting his anger on them. Enormous raindrops were falling now, soon the whole yard would be awash.

'Leave them,' said Charmian. She herself was getting wet. 'The rain will do them good.'

179

He muttered something hard to hear and went on pulling and shoving at the pots. He appeared angrier at Elspeth than seemed necessary, there was real fury in his face.

'Here, let me help.' It was a new side to Jerome, she had never seen him like this before.

'Leave it,' he ordered sharply.

Thunder was rolling round the sky, the rain coming down now in a steady sheet, hitting the ground like bullets. The soil in the pot she was moving was being stirred around like porridge.

Her foot went into a puddle, she slid forward and in steadying herself her hand plunged into the soft mud.

Her fingers touched something under the soil. She withdrew them with a frown. Her fingers were muddy and under the nails was a line of muck, dark and thick, that smelt. It smelt sickly sweet and corrupt.

She let the pot go. It tilted sideways and the mud shifted. She could see something brown and round, like a turnip. Only it was bigger and there was hair.

A gleam of teeth.

She was looking at a human head.

'I told you to leave it alone,' said Jerome.

Charmian felt queasy, she swayed slightly. 'Who is it?' She might have said: Which one?

'I don't know. Not without looking.' He put his arm round her and dragged her into the shop, slamming the door behind them.

She leaned against it, breathing unevenly. 'Don't do anything stupid.' Shock and surprise had not had time to seep in yet, but both were there in the background all right.

'Don't worry. I'm not a murderer.'

She still felt sick, but she could talk. Keep him talking, she told herself.

'What's that outside then?'

'An execution. Justice. What every man's entitled to.'

'For what?'

'A death they arranged.'

180

'Oh come on, they were both doctors. Whose death?'

'My wife's death. Oh yes, it was their fault. I hold them responsible. She was under Dr Cook while she was pregnant. He said it was a difficult pregnancy and sent her to hospital. To the woman, that woman Rivers, she took charge. Lisa had the baby all right but afterwards she started to bleed. Then they said she must have a hysterectomy. But she died a week later anyway. She never really came round. They said it was bleeding in the brain. But I knew that wasn't it. Just a cover-up. It was them. Their fault.'

'Oh I don't think so.'

'I couldn't prove anything, of course. You never can. I could have killed them then. But once that girl had the abortion I knew what I had to do.'

Charmian felt chilled. Between your understanding and mine, there is a gulf, she thought. 'How did you know?'

'Drove her to it, didn't I? I was their tame taxi, they often used me. And I collected her the same day. She was as bright as could be, talking about her holiday. It meant nothing to her. That did it. I made up my mind and just waited my chance. They were as good as dead when I drove them to Heathrow.'

'"The brothers and their murdered man",' said Charmian.

'What's that?' he asked suspiciously.

'A poem, by John Keats. "Isabella, or The Pot of Basil."' Geraniums in your case, she thought. 'Are you making a confession?'

'Well, it's not a dying speech. On the other hand, you've got no witnesses.' Then seeing her face, he said: 'Oh don't worry. You won't have to take me in. Or try to. The local lads have been snooping around the Yard. They've got to me somehow.'

Laraine? thought Charmian. He had pointed the finger at her in the beginning and now she was pointing it back. But the police must have had other indications.

'Pretending to have a general look round. I saw them in my car. Bound to have traces. They'll be back.'

'You didn't kill them in the car?'

181

'No, in the Rivers woman's house. Took her in with her luggage, like a proper taxi man, then stabbed her in the house while he waited in the car. Then I went back and got him. Told him she'd collapsed. Which she had. . . . I did the rest of the job there.' He gave Charmian a quick look to see if she understood. 'I'd brought the sacks with me from the Yard. . . . Afterwards, I dropped the cases out at the farm. Used to play there when I was a kid.'

The cutting up of the bodies, the disposal of the parts with the flour on them she knew about. More or less.

'I left the legs outside Dr Cook's surgery. A pointer for the lads.' He laughed. 'I ought to have known the gods were against me when they fetched up here. That Elspeth.'

'Why did you keep the heads?'

'For myself,' he said, and laughed again.

Like Isabella after all, she thought. Too much grief has driven you mad.

'Where's the baby?'

'With his grandmother.' He added reluctantly, as if not wanting to admit any imperfection on his perfect child, 'He's got the chicken-pox. And you'd better melt away before the boys in blue arrive, so they won't think you fancy me.'

Charmian flushed awkwardly. There were things better left unsaid. 'I'll stay. More professional. And they won't think that, because I'm going to give them a telephone call.'

'Suit yourself.' He watched her go to the telephone, even listened to her words and remained calm, as if it was no longer of interest to him. He knew what lay ahead of him, none better. He had probably made an estimate of his likely sentence and understood how ex-policemen fared in gaol. But he was satisfied: justice had been done. And then they both sat down to wait. The storm was passing over, soon the skies would be clear.

A few days later Charmian was walking down Peascod Street back from a lunch in the Castle with Lady Oriel. She knew now

182

that she would be settled in Windsor for a few years anyway. She had taken a lease on the flat in the Yard and was sending for her own furniture. Humphrey had asked her to marry him and she had refused. So that was out of the way. For the time being. Lady Oriel said she was wise. 'Let him stew,' she had said. 'Thinks too well of himself anyway.'

'I'll go on with my thesis,' Charmian thought, pausing for another look at the antique shop. The cradle had gone. Perhaps Elspeth had bought it. Certainly it would not have been Dolly Barstow even though she had announced that she planned to marry Dr Lennard. 'I owe them that. I want to show that there is no special sort of situation in which a woman will turn to crime where a man may not. There is no woman criminal as such, just people. Persons.' She promised herself, I'll go on knowing that lot if they'll have me. Even Laraine. Perhaps most of all, Laraine. Alas for Laraine, Delaney had been caught too, having made the mistake of leaving his plane on stopover in New York from where he would eventually be extradited.

Down the street ahead of her she saw a figure that seemed familiar. A young woman in jeans with a soft, much scuffed bag slung over one shoulder and a bouncy cheerful walk.

She hurried forward, and tapped her on the shoulder. 'Kate!'

The girl swung round, frowning. Then her face cleared. 'Godmother! How lovely. What are you doing here?'

Looking for you, among other things, thought Charmian. But she said: 'Where have you been?'

'Living in a cave with Harry. "Cave", French, a sort of basement place he rents in the Dordogne. We had to be alone. We were working things out.'

She saw Charmian looking at her battered luggage. 'I don't usually travel like this.' She was her mother's daughter after all, possessions had to be excellent. 'I lent my good stuff to a friend. Girl I was at school with, she works in a hospital here. I'll get it back.'

If you want it, thought Charmian, and wondered if she ought to tell her about Amanda, but she decided against it. Let her

183

find out. A shock might be good for Kate.

'Your father will kill you,' said Charmian.

'But I've left Harry. We were bad for each other. We brought out violence in each other. I might have killed him. Once I saw it clearly I just left.' Her face was bright and self-assured. 'It was easy.'

There was trouble ahead for a girl like Kate, decided her godmother. We haven't seen the last of what she can do to us.

'You just have to know who you are,' said Kate. 'Then, like I said, it's easy.'

Charmian said to her: 'How old are you, Kate?'

'Twenty-two.' A happy look came on her face. 'Just. I had a birthday and sent you all flowers.'

Charmian looked at her with amusement and sympathy mixed. 'It gets harder,' she said.